Ro. 2

Alta caught sight of him and blushed.

"P-Preacher, I didn't know you were here."

Jonas met her gaze with a soft smile. "I wanted to see how you were feeling. Your sister said you're doing better."

She bobbed her head before she took a big gulp of her coffee then gasped at the heat of the brew.

"Please sit, Alta," Jonas invited as he rose and pulled out a chair next to his. "Relax and enjoy your coffee. I'm not a scary man, but I guess you'll have to be the one to judge for yourself." He kept his tone light and teasing.

To his amazement, she blinked as if momentarily stunned then she chuckled. "What if I'm not a *gut* judge of character?"

The transformation of her beautiful features struck him like a blow to his heart. He quickly controlled his thoughts. "Lovina has known me for years. Ask her if you're wondering what type of man I am."

Alta met her sister's gaze.

"I can vouch that he's a *gut* man," Lovina said with a grin.

To Jonas's surprise, Alta smirked. *"Okey."*

Rebecca Kertz was first introduced to the Amish when her husband took a job with an Amish construction crew. She enjoyed watching the Amish foreman's children at play and swapping recipes with his wife. Rebecca resides in Delaware with her husband and dog. She has a strong faith in God and feels blessed to have family nearby. Besides writing, she enjoys reading, doing crafts and visiting Lancaster County.

Books by Rebecca Kertz

Love Inspired

Loving Her Amish Neighbor
In Love with the Amish Nanny
The Widow's Hidden Past

Women of Lancaster County

A Secret Amish Love
Her Amish Christmas Sweetheart
Her Forgiving Amish Heart
Her Amish Christmas Gift
His Suitable Amish Wife
Finding Her Amish Love

Lancaster County Weddings

Noah's Sweetheart
Jedidiah's Bride
A Wife for Jacob
Elijah and the Widow
Loving Isaac

Visit the Author Profile page at LoveInspired.com for more titles.

The Widow's Hidden Past

Rebecca Kertz

LOVE INSPIRED
INSPIRATIONAL ROMANCE

LOVE INSPIRED®
INSPIRATIONAL ROMANCE

Recycling programs
for this product may
not exist in your area.

ISBN-13: 978-1-335-58633-9

The Widow's Hidden Past

For questions and comments about the quality of this book, please contact us
at CustomerService@Harlequin.com.

Love Inspired
22 Adelaide St. West, 41st Floor
Toronto, Ontario M5H 4E3, Canada
www.LoveInspired.com

Printed in U.S.A.

Remember ye not the former things,
neither consider the things of old.
—*Isaiah* 43:18

For my cousin, Linda J. Barnes, with love.

Chapter One

Autumn, the Village of Happiness,
Lancaster County, Pennsylvania

"How could you! How could you betray your *dochter*?"

Alta Hershberger gazed at her oldest daughter with tears in her eyes. "I didn't, Mary. I didn't betray you! I wouldn't do that to you or Sally."

"I confided in you and you told everyone! Sally heard it from Aunt Miriam who heard it from members of her quilting bee. Now everyone knows that I had a miscarriage, and they all think that Ethan and I are having problems!"

"But you're not! I know how much your husband loves you."

Mary kept shaking her head. "I can't believe this. You've ruined everything! Now everyone is talking about Ethan and my personal business!" Tears ran down her face, making Alta's stomach clench to see her daughter in pain. "I won't forgive you for this! I can't." The last was whispered before Mary ran out the door, crying.

"Mary, wait!" Alta jumped up from her kitchen chair. She would make Mary understand that she'd never said a word about Mary's miscarriage to anyone…and she certainly wouldn't have talked about Mary and Ethan's marriage. Mary was her child. She loved her and her younger daughter Sally. The fact that Sally was married to the bishop only made the gossip she'd supposedly spread more believable because Sally had confirmed that Alta had nattered. If the bishop's wife said that her mother had spread the gossip, then everyone would believe it was true.

Except it wasn't.

She ran outside to catch her daughter before she left. "Mary, please! I didn't do this. You must believe me!"

Mary paused near her buggy. "I don't. You have always been a busybody, and we never liked it, but we loved you because nothing you nattered about hurt anyone. Until now!"

Her daughter climbed into her buggy and steered the vehicle toward the road.

"Mary, please! Mary!" Alta chased after the buggy, hoping her daughter would stop and listen to the truth. But Mary kept driving, ignoring her mother's plea.

"Mary!" Alta tripped and fell hard. She lay a moment on the dirt driveway as her tears fell and ran down her cheeks. She struggled to rise and cried out at the excruciating pain in her hip. "Mary," she whispered as she pushed to her feet, watching Mary disappear. "I didn't do it."

But her daughters didn't believe her, and she knew that no one else would. She managed the two steps into the side door of her small house, where she and John had lived since they'd married. Thoughts of her late husband made her cry harder as she grabbed a chair and sat down. "I'm sorry, John. I've failed our daughters. What do I do now?"

By the end of the week, Alta realized that everyone within the community refused to acknowledge her. It was as if she were shunned. She decided that she needed to get away from Happiness. But where could she go? The only other family she had was her estranged sister Lovina, who'd been angry with her since the day that John had asked Alta to marry him and she had accepted. Lovina had been in love with John. Lovina had accused her of stealing her man, then she'd moved away and never returned. Alta had written to her sister numerous times, hoping for a reconciliation, but her letters were returned to her, unanswered.

Should she try again? Alta had recently learned that Lovina was living in New Berne. She packed her clothes and made sure the water was off in the house in case the weather turned cold. Then she locked up before she left and headed toward New Berne, Pennsylvania—and her sister.

Jonas Miller set the coffeepot to heat on the stove, then started to make his breakfast. He'd learned to cook after his wife's death. He had five children—three sons and two daughters, all of them grown but his daughter Fannie, who still resided with him. Fannie was an independent business owner who had worked hard to open a luncheonette. Her business was booming, and he had a feeling that it wouldn't be long before she met a man who wanted to court her.

He sighed as he scrambled eggs in a pan then turned three slices of bacon in another. There were times like now when he felt lonely. He was frequently invited to his children's houses for meals and Visiting Day, but while he loved every one of them, spending time with them didn't bring him the same comfort his wife Lena had given him when she'd been alive. He and Lena had enjoyed a good, solid marriage, and he'd missed her terribly since her passing. At first, the church elders had encouraged him to remarry, but he hadn't found a woman he wanted to wed, and he didn't want an arranged marriage. At nearly fifty years old, he figured he had a right to choose the woman he wanted to spend the rest of his life with. And he hadn't met her yet. He'd waved the elders' concerns aside and hoped for the best. Recently, however, he had been asked to be a minister in the church, and he was afraid that the elders would insist that he take a wife.

Jonas took both pans off the heat then opened the refrigerator to look for ketchup for his eggs. He frowned when he realized there wasn't any. Lena had always made sure he had everything he needed, he recalled with fondness. He was lonely without a wife, he admitted, but he was fine. He took stock of the refrigerator's contents and realized that it was empty of the basics and his favorite foods. How could this have happened? *Because Fannie has been bringing me meals home from her restaurant.* Jonas sighed. He'd have to go grocery shopping today.

After pouring himself a cup of coffee, he sat down at the table to eat his breakfast and think about his day. He could shop this morning then have lunch at Fannie's Luncheonette later.

Jonas ate his eggs without ketchup and enjoyed his crispy bacon with his coffee. When he was done, he cleaned up the kitchen and then made a list of the groceries he needed to purchase. "Everything," he murmured. "What don't I need?" By the time he left the house, he held a long list.

Minutes later he was on his way to Kings General Store to grocery shop. He had driven his wagon about a mile or so down the street when he saw a horse and buggy at an awkward angle on the side of the road near a farm. Jonas furrowed his brow. Was there something wrong? He pulled up behind the vehicle and got out. Approaching from the farm side of the carriage, he went up to the window and peered inside. A lone woman sat in the driver's seat with her head tipped toward her lap. He heard her sniffle and realized she was crying.

"*Hallo,*" he said softly, hoping he wouldn't scare her. "Do you need help?"

At the sound of his voice, she gasped and lifted a bright green gaze to meet his. He gave her a warm, encouraging smile. "I saw you stopped here and worried that something was wrong," he said. "Are you *oll recht*?"

She blinked rapidly, and he saw the telltale sign of her tears. She glanced away and wiped her eyes. "I'm fine," she said, looking at him again.

He arched an eyebrow. "Is there something I can do to assist?"

She nodded. "I'm trying to find Lovina Schlabach. Do you know where she lives? I've stopped and asked at a few businesses in town, but no one seems to know her."

Jonas eyed her with concern. "I'm afraid I don't know any Schlabachs who live here in New Berne." The woman was older than he'd first thought, he realized. She was lovely, with blond hair and green eyes the color of a lawn covered with dew on a bright morning. From the tiny lines at the outer corners of her eyes, he guessed she was in her forties and about four or five years younger than he was.

The woman's shoulders slumped. "I don't know what to do. I came here to see my sister, and now I have no idea where she lives." She closed her eyes, and he thought she might be fighting tears.

"You said your sister's name is Lovina?"

She nodded. "*Ja.* I…haven't seen her in years…" With a sigh, she glanced away as if she struggled with what to do.

"Lovina King lives close by. Maybe she's your sister."

The woman looked at him with hope. "Could

be she married, I guess." She seemed embarrassed that she didn't know.

"You can always visit the house to find out," Jonas suggested. He gestured in the direction her buggy was headed. "Continue straight on this road until you come to Kings General Store. You can't miss it. Make a right about a quarter mile past the store then continue along until you see a sign advertising eggs for sale. Lovina King lives in the farmhouse. She raises chickens and sells eggs."

The woman's green eyes studied him with gratitude. "*Danki.* I'll do that."

He stood a moment, unable to tear his eyes from her pretty face. When the woman blushed, Jonas realized he was staring at her. He blinked and smiled. "I should be going," he said. "I'll pray that Lovina King is your sister."

She flashed him a wide, genuine smile, so bright it filled his heart with a warmth like sunshine. He returned to his vehicle and watched as she carefully drove her buggy back onto the road. Jonas followed moments later and caught sight of the rear end of the woman's carriage as he reached the general store. He hoped she'd be all right, he thought as he pulled into the parking lot. The memory of the vulnerable woman's sad eyes and then the smile that had transformed her features were etched in his mind. Although he may not see her again, he couldn't help but wonder about her and pray that she'd be all right.

Alta Hershberger was nervous as she steered her buggy past Kings General Store toward the road she needed to turn on in order, she hoped, to find her sister. If it was her, would Lovina still be angry with her after all these years? It had been over twenty-six years since they'd last seen each other, and their parting had been awful. If Lovina King was, in fact, her only sibling, then her sister had married. Was she happy? Would Lovina ever forgive her for marrying the man she'd loved?

Tears filled Alta's eyes as she reflected on the sixteen wonderful years that she'd enjoyed with her husband Johnathan before he'd passed away. She'd given birth to their daughter Mary nearly two years after she and John had wed. Their youngest Sally had come a year later. They'd been happy together—John and she with their baby daughters. Alta had been living the life she'd always wanted with the man she loved and the children they'd created together. Then tragedy had hit when John suffered a fatal injury in a buggy accident when their girls were in their early teens. When he'd died, Alta had been afraid to drive a buggy for a long time afterward. She'd become over-protective of her daughters, fearing that she'd lose them, too. Alta had lost the love of her life, and she'd had difficulty facing a future without her husband. She'd wanted to crawl into bed and fade away, but her girls had needed her, so she'd faced each day as a challenge to be a good mother to Mary and Sally.

The road she was looking for appeared on the right. Thoughts of her recent problems with her community were superseded by her increasing nervousness at encountering her angry sister again—if the woman *was* her sister. She could hear the voice of the man she'd just met, recalled the warmth in his brown eyes, and garnered the courage to do this. Alta saw the egg sign near the road that the kind man had told her about. She flipped on her blinker and made the turn onto the long dirt lane that led up to a large farmhouse situated far off the road.

"Dear Lord, if this is my sister, please let her forgive me," she prayed aloud as her vehicle bumped over a few ruts in the dirt lane. "I'll work hard to be a better person. I'll do whatever I can to put You, Father, above everything."

The King residence was well maintained, she saw, as she parked her buggy in the barnyard. A woman came out of the house and waved. Alta took a long look at her and recognized that this Lovina was indeed her sister. She could feel her heart pumping hard in her chest. Her hands felt clammy, and she was afraid she would pass out.

"Hallo!" her sister called out as she approached with a smile. "Have you come for eggs?"

Bracing herself for rejection, Alta opened the buggy door and climbed out. Their gazes met. Lovina froze and stared at her, as if unable to believe her eyes.

"Alta?" Her sister appeared stunned.

Alta drew in a sharp breath and nodded. *"Ja,* it's me, *schweschter."*

As her sister came closer, Alta saw that Lovina looked wonderful. "I'm surprised to see you." She looked toward Alta's buggy as if searching inside. "Did Johnathan come with you?"

Alta shook her head as a painful lump lodged in her throat. *"Nay,* he is no longer with us. I lost him eleven years ago." While her community looked at her as a busybody, she'd never shared any news with the *Budget,* the newsletter that many Amish communities subscribed to and read.

Eyes filling with tears, her sister regarded her with sympathy. "Come in and have some tea."

She swallowed hard. "You'll have me in?"

"*Ja,* 'tis been a long time. I wondered if I'd ever see you again. We can catch up."

A little of the tension left Alta's shoulders. "*Danki,* I would like some tea." She paused. "And to catch up."

When she entered her sister's house, Alta found Lovina's home warm and cozy. She detected the scent of chocolate. "It smells *wunderbor* in here," she said.

"Chocolate cake. My husband's favorite." Lovina smiled. "Sit, *schweschter.*"

As she took a seat, Alta experienced an intense curiosity to meet her brother-in-law. Lovina put a teakettle on the stove and turned on the flame. "Lovina, you look happy."

Her sister looked at her. "*Ja,* I'm extremely happy, more than I thought I'd ever be."

"I'm glad," Alta said sincerely. She had always felt terrible about the way she and Lovina had parted. She'd loved John, and after her sister had become upset with her for agreeing to marry him, she'd wondered if she should give him up. Alta had asked John before they'd married if he'd rather wed her sister. John had looked at her with warmth and affection. "*I love you, Alta, not your sister,*" he'd told her. "*You're the only woman I want as my wife and the mother of my children.*"

His sincerity had thrilled her—it still did

years later whenever she reflected on his feelings for her. She wished they could have enjoyed more time together. After the accident, she'd been angry at the driver who had hit John's buggy from behind. She'd never cried so much in her life as after her husband passed on, leaving her alone to raise their two daughters. Only once did the church elders press for her to marry, but they'd let it go after a problem she'd had with a prospective suitor. Thankfully, they had never urged her to wed again. John had been the love of her life, and no one could ever take his place. She'd received a hefty settlement from the driver's insurance company, so money hadn't been a problem for her. As for her daughters, they'd been old enough not to need a strange man as their stepfather. Their uncle Joseph had been all the male influence they'd needed in their life.

Lovina handed her a cup of tea.

Alta smiled at her and then took a sip. Her sister had remembered how she liked her tea—black with a tiny bit of sugar. She waited until Lovina had taken the seat next to her before Alta said what had been on her mind for years. "I'm sorry if I hurt you," she whispered, her eyes filling with tears. "I didn't know you had feelings for him."

Her sister nodded. "I know. In my heart, I

think I've always known, but I was so hurt at the time." She drank from her teacup. "You never tried to contact me."

"I wrote you three letters and all of them were returned. I figured you were still angry and wanted nothing to do with me." Alta wiped a tear off her cheek. "You'd moved first to Honeybrook, *ja*?"

Lovina inclined her head. "I stayed there for a year before I moved here to New Berne, where I met Adam, my husband."

A door slammed on the other side of the house.

"Mam, can I have something to eat?" A young boy of about twelve entered the kitchen from the great room.

"Didn't you eat breakfast?" Lovina asked.

"I can't help it if I'm hungry!"

Alta watched the boy as he interacted with her sister. His brown hair was ruffled as if he'd recently tugged off his hat. His green shirt brought out the gold in his brown eyes. His eye shape was her sister's, but the shape of his nose and his mouth he must have inherited from his father. Sensing her regard, the child looked at her. Lovina, recognizing her son's curiosity, smiled. "Alta, this is Isaiah, my middle *soohn*. Isaiah, this is your *endie* Alta, my sister."

Isaiah raised his eyebrows. "You have a sister?"

Lovina nodded. "We haven't seen each other in a long while. I'm hoping she'll stay with us for a time," she said, her gaze settling warmly on Alta.

"I'd like that," Alta replied, gratitude filling her heart.

"Can I have something to eat?" Isaiah's brown eyes seemed to plead with his mother.

"We'll be having lunch soon," Lovina offered as she rose to her feet. "Jonas is coming to eat with us. He'll be here in about two hours." She gave her son three cookies and a glass of milk. "That will have to do to hold you over, *soohn*."

Isaiah grinned, more than pleased with his snack, and left the room.

"That child is always hungry," Lovina said, "so I know the snack won't ruin his appetite."

Her sister set a plate of homemade cookies on the table between them and gestured for Alta to take some. Alta grabbed one and hesitated before taking a bite. "How many children do you have?" She nibbled on the cookie while she waited for an answer.

"Five," Lovina said with a smile.

"Five!" Alta blinked. "That's *wunderbor*."

"And you?" Her sister studied her with friendly curiosity.

"Two *dechter*."

Lovina's gaze softened. "How old were they when Johnathan passed on?"

Tears threatened and Alta blinked rapidly. "Fourteen and thirteen."

Regret filled her sister's expression. "Alta," she said softly, "I'm sorry for your loss. I had no idea."

"I'm…*oll recht*, but *danki*."

"How did you know where to find me?" Lovina took a bite of her cookie.

"I overheard my sister-in-law Miriam say that you had moved to New Berne." She drank from her teacup. She didn't mention the man who had pointed her in the right direction. If she hadn't caught part of her sister-in-law's conversation with Miriam's daughter Annie, Alta's niece, she never would have known where her sister lived.

"How is John's *schweschter*?"

Alta thought of the way Miriam had treated her before she'd left their Amish village of Happiness. How she and everyone within her community had believed the worst of her. "She is well," she said, fighting hard to hold back tears. She wouldn't say more as she'd made a promise to herself that she'd never again discuss another's personal business.

She watched as her sister took a pan with a

pot roast with vegetables from the refrigerator and put them in the oven.

An hour later the kitchen door behind Alta opened. "Lovina, do we have company?"

Alta turned as a man hung his hat on a hook on the wall before turning to smile lovingly at his wife. The delicious smell of the pot roast filled the room. "It smells *wunderbor* in here." He sniffed and closed his eyes as if pleased with the scent. He smiled when he saw Alta. "A newcomer," he said. *"Willkomm!"*

"Adam, this is Alta, my *schweschter*." Lovina turned to her. "Alta, my husband Adam."

Alta stood. "It's nice to meet you," she said, barely looking his way after her initial quick assessment of him. Her first glance at Adam had given her the impression of a handsome Amish man with blue eyes, brown hair and a touch of gray in his beard. She thought he must be a trustworthy, honorable man, considering how happy her sister was to be married to him.

Adam pulled out a kitchen chair and sat down. "Alta," he murmured, drawing her attention.

Alta met his brother-in-law's gaze. *"Ja?"*

"Why haven't you visited before now?"

"I... I wasn't sure I'd be *willkomm*."

His brown eyes softened as if he knew of the

rift between her and his wife. "You are family and will always be *willkomm*."

She released a shuddering breath. *"Danki."*

Lovina handed Adam a cup of tea. "Adam, Alta is going to stay with us for a while." She pushed the plate of cookies in his direction.

"That's *wunderbor*," he said.

Alta was overcome with emotion. *"Danki."*

Her sister smiled. *"Ja.* It's been too long since we spent any time together."

He smiled at Alta. "Have you met our *kinner* yet?" he asked as he grabbed a cookie.

"Only Isaiah."

Adam chuckled. "That child can be a handful, but he is a *gut* boy." He chewed and swallowed a bite of the cookie. "He's twelve and our middle one."

"The others should be home soon." Lovina studied her husband with affection. "You'll not let cookies spoil your appetite for our midday meal, will you?"

Adam reached out to pat his wife's arm. "Have you ever known me to skip a meal?"

To Alta's amusement, her sister blushed. *"Nay."*

"Well then." He leaned back in his chair as he drank his tea. His gaze returned to Alta. "We are truly blessed to have you with us,"

Adam said. He finished his cookie. "Do you have *kinner*?"

"She has two," his wife said.

Alta nodded. "*Ja,* two *dechter,* Mary and Sally. They are married and have their own homes."

"So, you and your husband live alone."

"*Nay,*" Alta replied quietly. "Only me. I'm a widow. My husband died a long time ago." She bit her lip. "Buggy accident."

Adam eyed her with compassion. "It's *gut* that you are here. You can learn about your sister's—and your—family, *ja*?"

Alta gave him a genuine smile before turning to flash one at her sister. "I...*ja*, that would be *wunderbor.*"

He turned to his wife. "Lovina, I saw Jonas and reminded him about lunch."

"You think he forgot?" Lovina refilled Alta's and her teacups.

"It's possible." Adam smiled. "But he seemed pleased to join us." He stood. "Lovina, I need to check on our Belgian. There is something wrong with his back leg. I'll keep an eye out for Jonas." Her brother-in-law grabbed his hat and exited the house through the back door.

"Jonas Miller is one of our ministers," Lovina explained. "You'll get a chance to meet a *gut* family friend and one of our church elders."

"I don't want to intrude on your gathering," Alta said. A church elder? She suddenly felt as if she shouldn't have come. She was unworthy to eat with a leader in the New Berne Amish church.

"Alta, you are one of us. Stay," Lovina said sincerely.

"What can I do to help?" Alta felt better but was still nervous about meeting Jonas Miller.

"The pot roast and vegetables will be ready soon. The chocolate cake I made is for dessert. If you could set the table for me, that would be great."

"I can do that." Alta was grateful for something to do. "For nine?" she asked, mentally calculating Lovina's family members and the minister as well as herself.

"*Ja,* nine." Lovina smiled at her. "There is plenty of food and room at the table."

The scents in the house were heavenly, making her mouth water. Alta examined the set table and was pleased with how nice it looked.

Adam entered the house. "Jonas's here," he announced as another man followed him inside.

Alta, curious, turned for a look at the newcomer's familiar face and gasped. *"You."*

Chapter Two

"Meet my *schweschter*, Alta Hershberger," Lovina said as she untied her apron and tugged it off.

Jonas grinned as he recognized the woman he'd encountered on the side of the road earlier. "I'm happy you made it—and that Lovina is the one you were looking for."

Lovina glanced with curiosity from him to her sister. "You've met?"

Alta nodded. "*Ja*. This morning when I asked him if he knew where you lived," she explained, her expression wary.

"I wasn't sure that you were Lovina Schlabach before you married Adam." The fact that he'd found Alta sobbing had made him feel bad for her. Jonas couldn't help smiling. It was wonderful to know that he had helped her when he stopped to see if she was all right.

"*Danki*, Jonas." Lovina looked pleased. "It's been a long time since Alta and I have seen each other, and I've missed her. I don't know if I would have found her if not for you." She gestured to the table. "Sit," she urged. "Jonas, I hope you brought your appetite."

"I did," he said with a chuckle. "It certainly smells *gut* in here."

Alta blushed and seemed to shift with embarrassment as Jonas stared at her. He was glad she was here. He took a seat next to Adam and watched as Alta quickly moved to transfer dishes of food from the counter to the large trestle table big enough for the family and several guests.

The couple's sons Jebidiah and Henry entered the kitchen. "We're starving," Jebidiah exclaimed.

Henry shook his head. "You're always hungry."

Adam and Lovina's daughters Linda and Esther entered the room as well, and introductions were made between the young women and their aunt. Jonas noted Alta's reaction to meeting her nephews and nieces. There was a vulnerability about her that tugged at Jonas as she smiled shyly at her sister's children. Then he realized that his continued attention to Alta seemed to be making her uncomfortable, and he glanced away.

"Jonas, would you begin the silent prayer before our meal?" Lovina asked as they sat down to eat.

"Hands down," Jonas said. Everyone at the table bent their heads and placed their hands on their lap. "Let us thank the Lord for our food." All was quiet as each person offered up thanks to the Lord. After a few minutes passed, Jonas rubbed his hands over his denim pants and lifted his head. "Amen," he murmured. The word signaled that it was time to eat, and a sudden influx of voices grew as plates of food were passed around the table.

"Preacher Jonas, may I please have the vegetables?" Isaiah asked.

"Certainly," Jonas said as he handed the boy the bowl of carrots, onion and potatoes that were cooked with the pot roast.

The conversation grew around the table.

"*Endie* Rachel asked if I'd like to help her and *onkel* Jed at the store starting next week," Linda said.

Esther gaped. "She asked me the same thing!"

Adam forked up another serving of meat. "*Dechter*, I imagine there will be some days that your aunt and uncle will need both of you.

Jed told me the store has been extremely busy lately."

"I wouldn't mind working there." Isaiah buttered a piece of bread.

"Your turn will come," Lovina smiled at her young son. She turned to Jonas. "How has your day been?"

"It's been a *gut* morning," Jonas said with a glance in Alta's direction. As he continued to look at her, her face reddened before she dipped her head down and forked up another bite of meat. He knew he shouldn't stare at her, but he couldn't seem to help himself. "Alta and I met, then I was able to get my grocery shopping done. Fannie has been bringing me meals from her restaurant, and I'm afraid I didn't realize how empty my cupboards were."

Her eyes on her plate, Alta shifted in her seat. "Alta?"

Alta started when her sister said her name. *"Ja?"*

Lovina frowned. "Are you *oll recht*?"

"Of course," she answered quickly.

"Why don't you tell us about your *dechter*?" Lovina suggested.

Alta hesitated as if she was uncomfortable sharing. "I have two—Mary and Sally. Both married *gut* men."

"Do they have children?" Esther said as she lifted her glass of iced tea.

"Sally has three. She married our bishop. Mary—not yet."

Jonas studied her. Did he imagine it or did her face turn pale when asked about her girls? She didn't seem to want to elaborate on the subject, a strange thing since most people enjoyed talking about their children and grandchildren.

"I hope we can meet them someday," Linda said. "I didn't realize we had cousins on *Mam*'s side."

Unable to take his eyes off her, Jonas observed the way her fingers trembled as she ran a hand across her nape. He could tell something was bothering her, but what? Aware that Alta hadn't seen her sister in many years, he sensed it was something more than spending time with the family that was making her nervous. And why after all these years did Alta come now to find her sister? Not that it wasn't wonderful that the two had connected again.

Everything about Alta had surprised him. He'd never been this intrigued by a woman. Jonas couldn't help but think that there might be a way he could help her. If only he knew what her issues were. The only way to do that was to get to know her.

During the remainder of the meal, Alta was

silent, except for occasional one-word answers.
Knowing that he would have to think about
how he could get to know her, Jonas stood.
"*Danki* for the *wunderbor* meal, Lovina," he
said. "Alta, it was lovely to see you again." He
saw her nod.

"You're *willkomm*, Jonas." Lovina rose from
her seat. "I hope you will join us again soon."

Jonas smiled. "I'd like that. *Danki*."

Alta appeared to have trouble meeting his
gaze as she stood. "*Gut* to see you again, too."
The sound of her voice was soft, nervous.

"Alta, will you be here for Sunday service?"

"She will," Lovina piped up, not giving her
sister a chance to say otherwise. She turned to
her sister. "We're hosting."

Jonas nodded. "I'll look forward to seeing
all of you here on Sunday then." His attention
settled on Alta a moment before he softened
his expression. The woman averted her eyes,
apparently unwilling to maintain eye contact
with him.

"Let me make you a plate of leftovers,"
Lovina said.

"It's not necessary."

"I know but we have plenty, and I'd like you
to have a meal for another day. I'm sure Fannie doesn't always make it home with food."

Jonas smiled warmly. "*Danki,* Lovina."

Lovina fixed him a plate while Alta began to clear the table. Accepting the meal, Jonas thanked his hosts and then acknowledged each one in the room's name before he left. As he drove home, he thought about his chance meeting with Alta and how he looked forward to seeing her again. He was determined to find out what was bothering her. There was something about her that drew him in. He wanted, needed, to alleviate the pain and fear he'd glimpsed in her beautiful green eyes.

Alta had difficulty sleeping the first night in her sister's home. She couldn't stop thinking about everything that had occurred in the last few days. Her mind spun with visions of her daughters along with others within her Amish community. While she was overjoyed that she and Lovina were speaking again, it had felt awkward for her to meet her brother-in-law Adam and their five children, knowing that Lovina's family learned how long it had been since she and her sister had seen each other. As she thought back on the time in her life when Lovina had left, Alta had been happy that she'd had Johnathan, the love of her life, but she'd lost her sister, which had upset her. And then her husband had died, and she'd lived her life for her girls. Remembering her last conversations with Sally and Mary was painful. Had she failed them? Been a horrible mother to them? Alta had tried to show her daughters how much she loved them, yet the girls—young women now—had been quick to believe the worst of her.

The knowledge of what happened and how she'd come to be in New Berne made her ashamed of the reason that she'd looked for Lovina. If her sister had rejected her, Alta hadn't been sure where she would have gone next, because she no longer felt welcome in her home village of Happiness.

Exhausted by her thoughts and her journey from Happiness to New Berne, Alta finally fell asleep. She woke with a start the next morning, fearful that she'd overslept. After dressing quickly, she went downstairs to find that the only people awake were Lovina and Adam.

Adam was the first to spy her in the kitchen doorway. "*Gut mariga*, Alta."

"*Gut* morning." Alta attempted to smile as she ran her hands down the front of her tab dress. "I'm sorry, *schweschter*. I should have been down sooner to help you."

Lovina frowned. "Why?"

"I'm a guest. There is no excuse for oversleeping." Alta approached her sister at the kitchen counter where she assembled ingredients for what Alta recognized as a breakfast casserole. "What can I do to help?"

"You arrived only yesterday, Alta," Lovina said. "You must be exhausted by your journey. You should have stayed in bed."

Alta shook her head. "I don't want to be an imposition." She shifted uneasily under her sister's gaze.

"I'm so sorry, *schweschter*," Lovina said softly. "For everything. I shouldn't have left. I could have been there for you after you lost your husband."

Allowing herself a small smile, Alta placed a hand on Lovina's shoulder. "Then you wouldn't have met Adam," she whispered.

"Still… I was awful to you."

"*Nay*, Lovina. You were hurting. That's something I understand."

"Did I hear someone mention my name?" Adam asked teasingly as he came up behind his wife and rested his chin for a moment on her shoulder.

Alta felt herself warming up to the two of them. "*Danki*, Adam, for taking *gut* care of my sister."

"She missed you, Alta," he said with a nod. "I'm grateful to have such a *wunderbor frau* and family. Now you're here and a huge part of us."

Alta blinked back tears at her brother-in-law's kindness and understanding. "I appreciate this more than you know."

"So, you had already met Preacher Jonas," Lovina said as Alta helped add the ingredients for a breakfast casserole.

"Ja." Alta cut up ham and crumbled cooked bacon for the dish. "I had asked workers inside several businesses if they knew where you lived, but no one had heard of you." She scraped the meat from the cutting board into a bowl. "I'd pulled over and wondered what I should do. Preacher Jonas stopped to see if I needed help. When I told him who I was looking for, he suggested that I visit Lovina King. I was relieved it was you."

"I'm glad he was able to assist." Lovina beat up eggs and added them to the bowl. "He's a good man, Alta. You're lucky he stopped. What would you have done if he hadn't?"

"I don't know," Alta answered. She couldn't go back to Happiness. "I would have looked elsewhere or…"

"Gone home?"

"Possibly," Alta said, although she knew that wouldn't have been likely. After opening the package of shredded cheddar cheese, she placed it on the counter. *I would have continued until I found a safe place to stay awhile.*

She watched Lovina pour the contents of the bowl into a large baking pan, and Alta sprinkled the cheese on top.

"What do *you* think of Jonas?" Lovina asked casually.

Alta felt a jolt and couldn't immediately find the words to reply. "He seems nice."

Lovina inclined her head. "He is. I like to have him over for a meal now and again. He lost his wife five years ago. Jonas has five *kinner*, but four of them have already moved out of the house. The only one left is Fannie, his youngest *dochter*."

"I'm sorry to hear of his loss." Alta turned her back on her sister to give herself a moment. She knew exactly how it felt to lose your other half. She wondered how old he was and decided it didn't matter. It wasn't like she'd be here long enough to get to know him. And he was a church elder while she was…unworthy. A mental image of her late husband came to mind. John wouldn't have been pleased with her. Her daughters were furious with her, and her community was upset because they believed she'd nattered. And there wasn't anything she could do to alter or change her situation back home.

Chapter Three

On church service Sunday, Jonas drove his buggy onto the Adam King property and parked it in the line of vehicles near the barn. The weather was beautiful with blue skies and warm sun. The beauty of the day alone would have made his morning, but today he would read a Bible passage and then talk about it afterward, both of which he enjoyed since he'd been ordained a minister.

After climbing out of his vehicle, Jonas skirted it to the other side to help his daughter with the cakes she'd made for the meal after service. He reached into the back of the buggy to hand Fannie two of the cakes then grabbed two to carry himself. As he and Fannie headed toward the house, he spied Alta with Lovina and Alta's nieces as they came out of the barn together. He felt a jolt as he studied her.

Alta will be staying with Lovina for an extended visit. A widow with grown daughters, Alta Hershberger was a lovely woman, but everything about her seemed sad—her expression, her quiet demeanor, her fear and inability to meet his gaze whenever he spoke to her.

Jonas didn't understand what it was about her that drew him in, especially since he hadn't been intrigued by a woman since his wife's death. His reaction to Alta was odd, perhaps caused by the knowledge that she'd lost her spouse, too. The woman continued to pique his interest. Was she still suffering from the loss of her husband, or was it something else?

"Who's the woman with Lovina?" Fannie whispered.

"That's Lovina's *schweschter* Alta. I was introduced to her the other day when I had lunch with the Kings."

Alta wore a royal blue tab dress with a white cape and apron. Her blond hair was neatly pinned beneath her white organza head covering. Lovina and her daughters were dressed similarly. He and Fannie paused and watched as the sisters entered the house. Lovina exited seconds later.

Catching sight of them, Lovina immediately headed in their direction. *"Hallo,* Jonas. Fannie.

It's *gut* to see you both. Fannie, your cakes look delicious. Jonas, may I carry those for you?"

"No need," he said. "I'll take them inside." He wanted to say hello to Alta.

Lovina nodded. "There is coffee on the stove—and muffins on the kitchen table if you're hungry. Help yourself."

Jonas smiled. *"Danki."*

Alta was shifting food containers from the counter to the refrigerator when he and Fannie entered the house. *"Gut* morning, Alta," he greeted.

Lovina's sister gasped and spun. "Preacher!" Her gaze fell on Fannie then shifted away.

"Alta, this is my youngest *dochter* Fannie. Fannie, this is Lovina's sister Alta Hershberger."

"Pleased to meet you," Fannie said, and Alta responded in kind.

Jonas held up his two cakes. "Where would you like us to put these?"

"On the counter." Offering a shy smile, Alta gestured toward where the other desserts sat waiting for after the midday meal.

He could feel her shy gaze on him as he set them down and then turned to watch as Fannie placed the two cakes she carried in the same area.

"Dat, I'm going to head outside," Fannie

said. "I want to have a word with Danny before church starts." She smiled at Lovina's sister. "Alta, it was lovely to meet you. I'm sure we'll have a chance to talk later."

Jonas took the large bowl of potato salad from the table and handed it to Alta after she made room in the refrigerator for it. "Danny is her *bruder* and one of my twins."

"*Danki,*" she murmured as she took the bowl from him.

"You're *willkomm*. It's *gut* to see you again, Alta."

Jonas heard her sharp intake of breath. "It's nice to see you, too, Preacher."

"Jonas," he invited.

Alta blinked. "Jonas." A small genuine smile played about her lips, enchanting him until her expression became guarded. "You have twin *soohns*?" she murmured as if it had just occurred to her what he'd told her.

He nodded. She was beautiful. "I should get over to the barn," he said, not wanting to make her uncomfortable with his extended time spent in her company. "I'll see you after service, *ja*?"

Alta bobbed her head, and Jonas left with the mental vision of her stunning features.

Jonas headed toward the circle of men near the barn, no doubt discussing business and the weather. Service would be starting soon, and he knew that their deacon, Thomas Troyer, would wait a while longer to ensure that everyone had a chance to arrive.

"Corn's coming in *gut*," Micah Bontrager said as Jonas joined them.

"*Ja*, won't be long before it's time for the harvest," Evan, Micah's father, agreed.

"Jonas, how is the milk business?" Aaron Hostetler asked.

"Going well enough," Jonas said with a grin.

Aaron scratched the side of his face. "Do you need any help?"

"Why do you ask?" Jonas knew that Aaron was in construction and wondered why the young man wanted to know.

Aaron took off his wide-brimmed black felt hat and resettled it on his head. "My *bruder* Nate is looking for some dairy farm work. He'll do it for free since he's interested in learning."

Jonas was thoughtful. "Have him stop by tomorrow. I'd like to talk with him."

The younger man agreed. "Monday it is then. I'll let him know."

"Nate's not here today?" Micah asked.

"Not yet, but he will be soon." At the sound of a buggy, Aaron glanced toward the lane and grinned. "There he is now."

"I could talk with him today, but I think it'll be better if I familiarize him with my operation first." Jonas pulled on the bottom edge of his black vest. Like the other men in his Amish community, he wore his white shirt with a black vest and black pants. He had black dress shoes and a black felt hat with a wide brim.

Preacher David Bontrager crossed the yard from the house with Deacon Thomas and entered the barn. As if their presence was a signal, everyone moved to gather inside the structure. Adam's barn offered a large open space big enough for the church congregation. Jonas started to follow the other men when he caught sight of Alta leaving the house. He watched her a moment until she hesitated as she locked gazes with him, and then she continued toward the barn. He turned and entered the building where he saw Danny and Davy, his two identical unmarried sons who shared a house and a business, already seated in the men's section. Jonas sat on a front bench close to the pulpit. As he waited for service to start, Jonas sought out Alta in the women's section. She sat with her sister and Linda and Esther, Lovina's daughters.

Alta's attention seemed focused on the lectern until she turned and met his eyes, her expression one of surprise when she caught him watching her. He was close enough to glimpse a flicker of uncertainty in her green eyes before she looked away.

The other preacher, David Bontrager, walked up to the pulpit and opened a book. Everyone stood to sing a hymn from the *Ausbund*. Jonas rose and left the room with the other church elders while the congregation continued to sing.

The elders entered a room in the house for a council meeting. They discussed who would address the community and talked about a family who needed help with medical bills. It was decided that a fundraiser would be the best way to go. Jonas offered to oversee it. As they walked across the yard to the barn again, Thomas Troyer, the church deacon, placed his hand on Jonas's arm to stop him.

"Several of our church elders feel it's time you marry, Preacher Jonas. We haven't pushed you for a while, but you've been alone too long."

"As I said before, I won't marry someone I don't love." Jonas felt the instant tension between his shoulder blades. "I can't accept an arranged marriage."

"How do you know you can't fall in love if you don't give another woman a chance?" the deacon said.

Jonas shook his head. "What I had with my *frau* was…" he began, distraught at the idea of replacing Lena.

"Was a long time ago, Jonas," Thomas

pointed out. "The bishop has brought this up to me again. I wanted to let you know."

Troubled by the brief unwelcome conversation, Jonas followed the church elders as they rejoined service. They arrived in time for the second hymn, the *Loblied,* and Jonas sang with the rest of the congregation. His enjoyment of the hymn was marred by worry. He knew the community expected him to remarry because of his obligation to God, but did they honestly believe that without a wife he couldn't discharge his duties properly? With eyes closed, Jonas offered a silent prayer for God's assistance before he felt calm enough to allow his deep voice to rise in song.

Something inside drew him to seek out Alta. Unable to keep his eyes from her pretty face, he saw that she sang with emotion in her expression, as if she took great pleasure in praising God. He felt himself grow calm. The Lord would help him. He just had to believe that all would turn out all right.

Preacher David went to the pulpit as the song finished. As everyone became silent, David gave the introductory sermon or *Anfang.* Then everyone prayed silently, some on their knees while others remained seated, especially mothers with young children.

The assembly stood and Jonas, who'd been

kneeling, rose and walked to the front of the congregation where he read from chapter one of James in the Bible.

"…If any of you lack wisdom, let him ask of God, that giveth to all men liberally, and upbraidth not; and it shall be given him. But let him ask in faith, nothing wavering. For he that wavereth is like a wave of the sea driven with the wind and tossed …"

At David's earlier request, Jonas said a few words about faith and being loyal to God. With each word he spoke, he felt God's love. With a silent prayer for the Lord's guidance, he returned to his seat as David continued with *Es schwere Deel*, the main sermon. Next came *Zeugnis,* testimonies to the main sermon from church elders, except for Jonas, including Preacher David. Three hours after the start of service, David gave the closing remarks. A prayer, an announcement and a final hymn signaled the end of the service. The youngest within the community left first, followed by others in order of their ages. When the women and children were gone, Jonas immediately got to work with the men to get ready for the midday meal. He went to the bench wagon and grabbed a table, watching briefly as Alta and the other women left the building for the main house to bring out the food. He set up a table inside the barn, then placed a church bench on each side of it, his mind filled with thoughts of Alta Hershberger. Offering up a silent prayer, he asked God to show him what was wrong with her so he could help her find peace.

Alta grabbed two side dishes for the midday meal and then crossed the yard to one of two tables inside the barn. She saw Jonas as soon as she entered. He was shifting some of the dining tables to make more room for the benches. Seeing the man at the pulpit, hearing his deep voice as he'd read from scripture and talked about the Bible verse he'd chosen had affected her like nothing before. She felt sure he was a kind and honorable man and was relieved.

God had sent him to assist her with directions to Lovina's, she thought as she set a dish of cold ham and a bowl of chow-chow on the food table. Her gaze settled on Jonas briefly before she returned to the house. She couldn't help but be curious about him as she entered Lovina's kitchen to fetch more food.

"Alta," Lovina said, "would you take out the plates and utensils?"

Alta nodded then reached for paper plates, plasticware and cups for the iced tea she'd made yesterday afternoon.

Her nephew Henry entered the house.

"*Soohn,* will you get one of your *bruders* to help carry out the iced tea jug?" his mother asked.

"*Ja, Mam,*" he said and left the house, returning within moments with his younger brother Isaiah.

Alta followed her nephews to the barn and watched as the boys carefully set the jug on top of a table. She placed the cups next to the jug and the plates with utensils at the other end. When she went to turn, she stumbled and twisted her leg. Gasping with the pain in her hip, she straightened herself and tried not to make it obvious she had hurt herself as she left the barn. Once outside, Alta couldn't keep from limping. Her hip, which had just settled down from when she'd hurt it weeks ago chasing Mary's buggy, was back. She had reinjured it, and she wasn't sure how she would manage without anyone's notice.

She drew a sharp breath to prepare herself for climbing the stoop to the house. Alta wondered if Lovina would have anything that might help her, like ibuprofen…or if her sister just used apple cider vinegar and water to ease aches and pains.

The women were outside. Somehow, she'd missed them bringing out the rest of the food. Alta entered the house and went into the great room where she sat for a moment. Closing her eyes, she fought tears. And it was there that he found her. Jonas Miller.

"You hurt yourself," Jonas said. "I saw you limping. Is it your foot?"

Alta opened her eyes and felt nervous as she looked up at him. "*Nay,* it's my hip." She couldn't help but notice how handsome the preacher was with his brown hair and beard. His brown eyes were full of compassion, and she experienced a funny little quiver inside whenever she looked at him.

"You're hurting."

She drew a sharp breath. "Give me a moment," she whispered, "and maybe the pain will subside." When he continued to eye her with concern, she explained, "I hurt it a couple of weeks ago. I was feeling better until I stumbled and landed the wrong way." Alta swallowed hard as she tried to get past the sharp throbbing ache, closing her eyes. It felt awkward to have this man see her like this. "I'll be fine." But then she shifted and winced. "Or it may take me a little longer to feel better."

"You need to take something," he said gently. "Acetaminophen or ibuprofen. I think Lovina has some in the kitchen. I saw Linda on the way in. I'll ask her where her *mudder* keeps them."

Before Alta could object, Jonas left. He returned within minutes with a glass of water and two capsules. "Ibuprofen," he said as he handed them to her. "If you don't feel better in a day or so, you may want to see a doctor. I can take you there if you'd like."

Embarrassed, Alta regarded him with dismay. "Not necessary," she told him. "I'll be *oll recht*."

"We'll see." His warm smile made her heart pound. "Let me help you, and we can join the others." He moved to take her arm.

Alta resisted. "You go. I'll be fine here by myself."

"Nonsense," he said. "You need to eat. If you want to rest here, that's all well and *gut*, but I'll be back with a plate for you." He turned to leave.

"Jonas!" she called, desperate to get his attention.

He halted and looked back. *"Ja?"*

"You don't have to go to all this trouble," she said, upset that he'd seen her at her worst. "I'm not worth it." She murmured the words, but his response suggested he heard it.

Jonas furrowed his brow. "I'll be right back."

She watched him walk away and felt bad for having him cater to her. It wasn't right. But he was a nice man and that was what men like him did.

Alta had her eyes closed when she heard him return. She lifted her eyelids, saw the plates and couldn't help grinning. "I hope you plan on sharing that food with me. You brought enough to feed several people!"

He held a ceramic plate filled with roast beef, a mixture of pickled garden vegetables called chow-chow, macaroni salad, pickles, potato salad and a separate plate with a slice of chocolate cake.

With a chuckle, he sat in the chair next to hers. "We could eat in the kitchen, but I think it would be better if you ate it here."

"Or on the front porch," Alta suggested.

Jonas beamed at her. "*Wunderbor* idea." He stood, set the dessert plate on the chest of drawers against the wall and then, with the other plate in his hand, he reached to help her up.

Blushing, Alta gazed at his large masculine hand a moment before she grabbed hold. His fingers felt warm and strong around her own. As she rose, she winced.

"Maybe we should stay here," Jonas said when he saw her struggle. "I don't want you to injure yourself further."

"I'll be *oll recht*," she assured him as she stood a moment to get her balance. He had shifted his hold from her hand to her arm. His grip was sure and gentle as he held her while he waited for her to feel steady enough to move.

"Alta?" Lovina's voice came from the kitchen.

In the great room!" she called.

Within moments, her sister entered the room and stopped abruptly when she saw Alta standing with Jonas's aid. Alta felt her face heat. By an unspoken exchange, the man faced her sister as he lowered Alta into the chair.

"She hurt herself," Jonas said with concern.

Lovina immediately looked worried. "What's wrong?"

"My right hip," Alta said, "but I'll be *oll recht*. I hurt it a few weeks ago, and it was much better but then I twisted my leg in the barn when I went to turn."

"What happened? How did you first hurt it?" her sister asked.

"I fell in my driveway back home." She shifted and gasped. "Jonas, it was kind of you to bring me food. I'll be fine by myself."

"Nonsense," Lovina said. "Why don't you come into the kitchen? You'll be more comfortable at the table." Her gaze settled on the plate in the preacher's hand. "With everyone in the barn, no one will bother you there." She watched as Jonas grabbed the dessert plate so both of his hands were full.

Alta nodded. She started to push herself to her feet, but the pain in her right hip made her woozy. Jonas quickly handed Lovina the two plates and then carefully assisted Alta to her feet. "I'm sorry," she murmured to her sister and Jonas. "I don't mean to be a burden. I'm sure I'll be fine in a little while."

Lovina watched with concern as Jonas helped her to a kitchen chair. "Why don't you eat then lie down for a bit?"

"Nay," Alta said, shaking her head. "I want to help you put the food away later."

"Alta," Jonas objected, his deep voice a vibration like a hum down her spine.

"Don't worry." She managed a smile. "If I'm not better soon, I'll rest." He looked relieved and so did her sister. "Please go outside," she urged them. "I won't do anything to aggravate this."

"Let me get you something to drink," Lovina offered.

She shot her a grateful look. "That would be *gut. Danki.*"

"Are you sure you'll be *okey*?" Jonas seemed hesitant to leave her.

Lovina rewarded him with a smile. "I'll check on her in a little while." Yet he stayed while Lovina poured her a glass of lemonade from the refrigerator. "There you go," she said. "You won't have to be alone long."

Alta nodded, overly aware of Jonas's continued presence. "*Danki* for your kindness, Preacher," she said.

He frowned at her mention of his title. Then he nodded as if he understood. "Take care of yourself, Alta. I hope you feel better."

After her sister and Jonas left the house, Alta grew tearful. But then she drew herself up. She felt worse rather than better after Jonas's and her sister's kindness, as she didn't deserve it. And coming so soon after her community wanted her to leave, she felt emotional as well as physically in pain.

Please, Lord, help me get better quickly so I can help my sister and her family. I don't want to be a burden. She didn't want to do something that would cause Lovina to be sorry that she'd asked her to stay.

As she thought of Jonas, she prayed harder. *Father, don't let Jonas discover the truth about what happened between me and my girls.*

Chapter Four

Jonas worried about how Alta was feeling since Sunday when he saw her limping. Did she see a doctor? *She's an out-of-town guest who will be going home.* The fact that he couldn't stop thinking about her gave him pause.

The wind picked up as he drove his horse-drawn buggy closer toward Adam King's property. He wondered how well Alta was settling in with her sister's family. While he could tell that she was glad to be there, something in her expression at odd moments had convinced him there were secrets behind her beautiful green eyes—secrets that upset her. Would she ever confide in him? He was a patient man, and he would wait until she was comfortable with him. Jonas hoped she wouldn't leave before he could earn her trust.

It was a clear Tuesday morning, and Jonas

was glad he finally could get away for a visit. He would have checked on Alta yesterday, but he'd needed to get things done on his dairy farm that couldn't wait. By the time he'd met with Nate Hostetler and finished his work for the day, it was late, and he hadn't wanted to disturb the King household during suppertime.

The residence loomed on the left. Jonas drove his buggy onto the property and parked close to the house. He climbed from his vehicle then reached in for the pie his daughter had brought home from her restaurant late yesterday after closing. Cradling the dessert carefully, he approached and knocked on the back door. Within seconds, Lovina answered it.

"Jonas! It's *gut* to see you! Come in," she said with a wide smile of welcome. "What do you have there?"

"Fannie's chocolate cream pie." He handed it to her then quickly looked about the room to discover that Lovina was alone. Jonas fought the disappointment at Alta's absence.

Lovina set the dessert on the countertop and then faced him. "Would you like a cup of coffee? I just made it. I was about to call Alta downstairs to join me."

"I would love a cup. *Danki*." Jonas's spirits lifted, a feeling he didn't want to interpret too closely on hearing Alta's name. He hung his hat on a wall hook then took off his light jacket and laid it across the back of a chair. "How is Alta feeling?" he inquired as Lovina set his coffee on the table.

"She's doing much better." Lovina placed another cup on the table. "I encouraged her to take ibuprofen regularly since Sunday evening, and her pain has been manageable. Alta has been helping me with housecleaning this morning. Nothing seems to keep my *schweschter* down for long." She frowned as she slid a sugar bowl in his direction. "Something is bothering her, Jonas, but whenever I try to find out what's wrong, she tells me she's fine." She paused. "Do you think you might be able to help her? Talk with her. Maybe she's afraid I'll judge her, but despite our past…" To his surprise, guilt entered her expression. "…I love my sister and want only the best for her."

Jonas cupped his mug and studied Lovina thoughtfully, noting the genuine concern in her blue eyes. "I don't know that she'll talk to me." He sipped from his coffee. "How long will she be here?"

"A month, at least. Longer if I have my way. I'm not sure how she'll feel about staying with us for that length of time. She has family back in Happiness. I hope I can convince her to stay by reminding her we have years to make up for." Lovina locked gazes with him. "Please think about it," she said before she left the room.

"I'll try. That's all I can do." Jonas heard Lovina in the foyer calling upstairs to her sister. He found himself staring at the doorway so he could catch sight of Alta before she realized he was here. Lovina entered the room first, and he averted his eyes. Then he sensed Alta's presence and glanced toward the open doorway where the kitchen met the rest of the house. She walked in, her attention immediately drawn to Lovina who was pouring a mug of coffee at the stove.

"I finished all the floors upstairs," Alta said, sounding pleased. "I'll do the dusting next."

Lovina turned from the stove and handed her sister a full coffee mug. "Don't worry about the dusting. You don't have to work so hard, *schweschter*. Sit down and enjoy your coffee with us."

"Us?" Alta spun, caught sight of him and blushed. "P-preacher, I didn't know you were here."

Jonas gave her a soft smile. "I wanted to see how you were feeling. Your sister said you're doing better."

She bobbed her head before she took a big

gulp of her coffee then gasped at the heat of the brew.

"Please sit, Alta," Jonas invited as he rose and pulled out a chair next to his. "Relax and enjoy your coffee. I'm not a scary man, but I guess you'll have to be the one to judge for yourself." He kept his tone light and teasing.

To his amazement, she blinked as if momentarily stunned, then she chuckled. "What if I'm not a *gut* judge of character?"

The transformation of her beautiful features struck him like a blow to his heart. He quickly controlled his thoughts. "Lovina has known me for years. Ask her if you're wondering what type of man I am."

Alta looked at her sister as Lovina took the seat across from him. "Lovina?"

"I can vouch that he's a *gut* man." Lovina grinned.

To Jonas's surprise, Alta smirked. *"Okey."*

Jonas stood after he'd finished his coffee. "Are you up for a walk?" He watched her as she hesitated before answering him.

"She's up for it," Lovina said with a glance toward her sister. "Don't look at me that way, Alta! You've been doing housework since before breakfast. Go. Enjoy the fresh air."

Alta's cheeks turned a bright shade of pink. *"Oll recht."*

"I won't keep you long," Jonas told her as she finished her coffee and then stood. "I need your help." Alta gave her sister a look, which would have been amusing if he hadn't known something was bothering her. He held the back door open for her and followed her outside. "Let's walk toward the back of the property."

Autumn had altered the landscape. The leaves on the trees were vibrant shades of gold, orange, yellow and red. If she appreciated the glorious view that was the height of the season, she didn't mention it. Alta remained quiet as she kept pace with him yet she somehow left a measure of distance between them. The silence was painful. Jonas was determined to make her feel comfortable with him.

"What did you think of church service last Sunday?" he asked softly, halting in the hopes that she would stop and look at him.

She paused. "It… I liked it." Alta glanced quickly away. "I especially liked the passage you read and what you said afterward."

"Danki." Jonas felt a flutter in his chest, a sensation he didn't ever remember feeling before. He touched her arm and felt her muscles tighten. He immediately shifted away and continued along the pasture fence to the right of the property until the farm fields were far behind them. "I'd like to ask you something," he ventured carefully.

* * *

"Oh? What?" Alta said, aware that her voice sounded odd, trembly, to her ears. Surprised that Jonas had asked her to walk with him, she felt a heightened sense of him as they strolled together along the line of trees her brother-in-law must have planted as a windbreak. Because of Lovina's ease around the man, she knew she had nothing to fear from him. Still, she couldn't help but be a little wary of him.

Jonas faced her, drawing her attention. "There is a family in our community—the Eshes. Their youngest son had to have an appendectomy two months ago, and there were complications. The boy—Hadley—is doing well now, but the medical bills are high, and his *eldra* need financial assistance."

Alta immediately felt sympathy for the Esh family. "How can I help?"

The man's smile was heart-melting. "I'm in charge of the fundraiser, which we hope to hold soon." The brown eyes beneath his wide-brimmed straw hat seemed to sear into her soul. "I was hoping you could help me with it."

"You want me to help you with a fundraiser?" she asked, stunned by his request.

He nodded. "I'd like to hear your ideas. I'm sure you've worked fundraisers before, *ja*?"

"I have." And it was something she was comfortable discussing with him. The fundraisers she'd worked on had been successful in her home community, and many families over the years had benefited from them. "Back in Happiness, we usually offered some type of meal for breakfast or the midday meal, offering the same food all day." She bit her lip as she gazed up at him. "What have you done in the past here?"

"We've held a breakfast, but I was thinking that those who attend might also like something sweet. I could ask Fannie to contribute. She owns a luncheonette and makes wonderful cakes and pies."

Alta smiled. "What if we offer breakfast food—pancakes and waffles as well as eggs and bacon or sausage? We can add chocolate chips to the pancakes and fruit toppings to the waffles. And maybe we add a table just for selling cakes, pies and other treats for people to take home? That would cover everything and be doable." She was pleased when his warm brown eyes lit up at her suggestions.

"That's a *wunderbor* idea, Alta." He grinned. "Would you be able to organize this with me? Then we can ask others to pitch in on the day of the event." She noticed his thick, dark eyelashes as he blinked several times while waiting for her answer.

"I'll be happy to help."

His wide grin created butterflies in her belly. "*Gut. Danki*, Alta. We can meet to discuss our plan during the week."

Alta felt an infusion of warmth spread through her head to her toes. *"Oll recht."*

The corners of his brown eyes crinkled as he continued to smile. "Shall we walk a little farther before we head back to the house?" He paused. "If you can spare the time."

She nodded then fell into step with him, following the tree line as they headed closer to the back of the property. They walked along the row of cypress trees.

"The sun feels good," Jonas commented. "Soon the weather will turn cold, and we'll be spending most of our time indoors."

Silently agreeing, she followed wherever he led her. "It's lovely here," she murmured.

Jonas inclined his head. "Is it nice where you're from? Happiness, is it?"

"Ja, it is," Alta said, trying hard to stifle the hurt she felt every time she remembered why she had to leave. "My favorite time of year there is spring. There are honeysuckles along the front of my *haus.* They look pretty in the summer and smell *wunderbor.*" She felt a jolt of homesickness but fought it, as she knew she couldn't return. At least not yet. Her thoughts

turned to Mary and Sally. Would they ever believe the truth? Did they miss her at all?

"We have honeysuckle bushes by my *haus*, too," Jonas said, drawing her attention back to the attractive man. He hesitated, and they walked in silence for a time. "Lovina explained that you're a widow. How long has it been?"

Alta averted her gaze. "A long time," she murmured. "Since my oldest was fourteen and my youngest thirteen."

Jonas halted, his hand on her arm stopping her. She could feel his eyes on her but she couldn't look up at him. "Aren't your girls married?"

"Ja." She pulled away and continued to walk.

"Then that means it happened—"

"Over eleven years ago," she confided.

Jonas captured her hand. "Alta…" He breathed out.

On the verge of tears, she spun, pulling her arm from his grip. "We should get back." Alta turned and started toward the house.

"Alta." Her name on his lips gave her pause. He sounded emotional, as if he understood.

Head down, staring at the ground, Alta stopped and waited for him to join her. He had no idea how hard it'd been to be a widow who'd been encouraged to remarry. "I'm not to be pitied," she said.

He moved to block her way. "I don't pity you."

Looking up, she saw his sincerity. "Then what? If you don't pity me, what are you thinking?"

His small smile grew. "I think you are a strong woman, and I respect how you managed all these years on your own."

Jonas studied the woman before him and witnessed a myriad of emotions flash across her face. Eleven years without a life partner, he thought with amazement. It had been less time since Lena passed on, and he often felt lonely, even with five children who frequently visited and checked on him. He decided it best to change the topic, for it was clear that her loss was upsetting to her.

Alta started to hurry back to the house.

"Alta! Slow down!" he called.

She halted, and he could see her shoulders tensing as he reached her.

"I'm sorry if I said something to offend you."

Blinking, she gazed at him as if confused. "You didn't offend me."

He tilted his head as he observed her lovely face. "Then why were you running away from me?"

Jonas heard her draw a sharp breath before

releasing it in a shuddering sigh. "I'm sorry. It's not you," she whispered, holding onto his gaze for a moment before glancing away.

"Is there anything I can do to help?" he said as he meandered with her back toward the house.

"*Nay* but *danki*." Alta gave him a shy smile, which he returned gently.

They reached the house and Alta headed for the back door. "Alta," he said, drawing her attention, "about the fundraiser. Thursday? Will you go with me to look at places to hold it?"

Her expression lightened. "*Ja,* I'll be happy to."

"*Gut.* I'll pick you up at ten in the morning. Will that work for you?" Jonas wanted to give her time enough to do what she felt she needed to do to help Lovina with morning chores, for he knew by her comments this morning that she intended on doing all she could to assist her sister.

"I'll be ready at ten, Preacher," she said.

"Jonas," he invited.

She blushed. "Jonas."

"Enjoy the chocolate cream pie I brought. Fannie made it, and her pies are delicious."

Alta nodded without a smile, then turned and entered the house. Jonas thought about following her but decided she needed some time on her own. If he were present too much in her life, she might pull into herself. It had been good to see her relax a little, even tease him a bit, until he asked too many questions, which brought her guard up.

Jonas looked forward to seeing her again. He couldn't rid himself of the memory of her gorgeous green eyes. *The eyes are often the mirror of one's soul.*

Chapter Five

On edge, Alta peered at the barnyard through her bedroom window as she anticipated Jonas's arrival. Soon, she would go with him to consider different places to hold the fundraiser for the Esh family. As the clock ticked closer to ten, the flutter inside her chest increased at the prospect of seeing him again. Jonas Miller was an attractive man with brown hair and a tiny touch of gray in his beard. And she shouldn't be noticing that.

Earlier that morning, before her sister had left to visit a friend, Alta had asked Lovina about possible places for the fundraiser.

"The New Berne firehouse might work," her sister had said. "And I'm sure you'll be visiting the New Berne Community Center as well as the VFW."

"What do you think will work the best?" Alta asked, curious about her sister's opinion.

"I don't know, Alta. I have a feeling that Jonas knows other places to visit. It's not up to me. You and Jonas will need to decide."

"Me?"

"*Ja,* you. He asked you to accompany him because he wants your input."

It was a rainy day, unlike the day Jonas and she had walked together when he'd broached the subject of the fundraiser to her. Alta wore her purple tab dress and decided to wear her black coat to help protect her from the rain. When it was close to the time Jonas was due, she went downstairs to wait for him near the back door in the kitchen.

"*Endie* Alta."

She turned to see Isaiah with a smile on his face as he held up a cupcake.

The boy had taken a bite and there was a trace of chocolate icing at one corner of his mouth. "Did you make these cupcakes?"

Alta grinned. "I did. Do you like them?"

"*Ja*, they are delicious," he said as he grabbed a second one before he quickly took a bite. "*Danki.*" He reached for another cupcake and handed it to her. "Didn't you taste them?"

Alta shook her head.

"Here. Try one," her nephew invited.

She blinked. "Why?"

Isaiah gazed at her with warmth. "Because I don't think you realize how *gut* they are."

Eyeing him with affection, she stepped away from the window, took the cupcake from him and nibbled on it. It tasted good, a delicious blend of fudge frosting and moist yellow cake. "Not too bad. I guess I'll have to bake more often while I'm here."

"You're not going home any time soon, are you?" the boy asked with candor. "We like having you here."

Alta felt the pinprick of happy tears. "I don't know how long I can stay, but I do like being here with all of you."

A rapping sound drew their attention. Before she could move, Isaiah answered the door. "Preacher Jonas. Are you here for *endie* Alta?"

Jonas stepped inside, looking a little wet but no worse for wear. In his hand, he held a closed umbrella. His smile was genuine. "I picked an awful day to do this, *ja*?"

"I don't mind the rain," Alta said, meaning it. "As long as it's not freezing rain because that can be dangerous." In the past, she wouldn't have agreed to spend time with a man she barely knew, but Jonas was a preacher and a good man. She felt safe with him.

"So, you're willing to head out and visit a

few places?" he asked, eyes bright with good humor.

Alta shrugged. "Why not?"

Jonas's smile was contagious, and she chuckled *"Gut."*

She grabbed her light all-weather black coat and slipped it on. Alta could feel Jonas's eyes on her as she reached for a pad and pencil. Facing him, she smiled. "I thought I'd jot down information about each place."

"Smart." Jonas opened the door, stepped outside then put up his large black umbrella. "I think it's slowing down, but I don't want you to get wet." He waited for her to join him. Alta was impressed when he made sure she was fully under the umbrella as he led her toward the passenger side of his buggy. He stayed until she was inside then skirted the vehicle where he closed his umbrella and climbed in. He turned on the battery-operated windshield wipers and running lights before he pulled away from the house.

"Where are we going first?" Alta asked after he'd driven off the property and onto the road. The rhythmic *swish* of the wiper on the driver's side of the front window was a calming sound to her.

He glanced in her direction. "I thought we'd

visit the firehouse, then move on to the New Berne Community Center."

Alta basked in the warmth of his gaze. "Will we have to pay for the use of them?"

He kept his eyes on the road because of the weather conditions. "*Nay,* the New Berne Fire Department won't charge us. We raise money for them with a mud sale every year."

Alta was familiar with mud sales. The Amish residents of Happiness also raised money for their local fire department through the sale of donated items. The events were called "mud sales" because they were held outside during the spring with days that were rainy more frequently than not.

"But what about the community center?" She relaxed and was at ease as he drove. Since John's death, she was uncomfortable at times as a passenger in someone else's vehicle.

Jonas shot her a glance. "The center is for all New Berne residents. If we explain the situation to them, they will allow us to use the facility for free."

Silent as they headed toward the firehouse, Alta couldn't help but notice Jonas's large hands on the leathers. He managed the horse easily and proficiently as he steered the mare down the side of the road, allowing cars and other motorized vehicles to drive past.

The firehouse loomed ahead on the right. Jonas flipped on the turn signal and pulled into the lot on the side of the building. The fact that there was a hitching post told her how much the New Berne Amish community was involved in their local volunteer fire department.

Jonas got out of the buggy and went to Alta's side. She blushed as he held out his hand and helped her onto the wet parking lot. Fortunately, the rain had stopped, but he still took the umbrella with him. Jonas opened a back door without knocking or ringing a bell before they went inside. The entrance led to the bays where three fire trucks were kept. A fireman was cleaning inside the cab of a ladder truck.

"Keller!" Jonas called, and the man spun then grinned.

"Jonas Miller!" He threw the towel he was holding onto the truck seat before he approached. "I've been expecting you." Keller reached out and shook hands with Jonas. The man's gaze settled on Alta. "Who is this?"

"Alta, meet Keller Johnson. Keller, meet Alta Hershberger, Lovina King's sister. Alta will be organizing the fundraiser with me."

"It's nice to meet you, Alta. I know your sister and her husband well."

The fireman's good humor made her grin. "It's nice to meet you, too, Keller." She studied the interior of the firehouse intently. "How do you know Jonas?"

"Jonas used to be one of us several years ago." Keller gazed at Jonas. "You can come back at any time," the firefighter said as he focused his attention on the minister.

Startled, Alta gauged Jonas's reaction to Keller's last comment. "You were a volunteer here in New Berne?" She was surprised to see color seep into his cheeks.

"A long, long time ago when my wife was alive," Jonas murmured, and Alta couldn't help but notice the brief flicker of pain in his brown eyes. As if he knew she was watching him, he locked gazes with her. "Keller, are you ready to show us the room you rent out? I'd like Alta to get a feel for it."

"Of course." Keller waved to her and Jonas to follow. He led them toward the back of a garage bay. The firefighter opened a door to reveal a large open space. Folded tables and chairs were stacked on the far side of the room. "We have plenty of tables and chairs for a fundraiser."

Alta liked that the tables and chairs would be there for the community to use. "It's a nice space," she said and she saw Keller nod. Alta faced Jonas. "What do you think?"

"This area is *wunderbor*, but the firehouse doesn't have much of a kitchen." He turned toward Keller. "I'll let you know before Saturday."

Keller nodded. "Take your time and look around. You said you wanted to hold the event in two weeks. A Saturday?"

"Most likely." Jonas gave Keller a nod and the man left.

Alta realized that there was no one else other than Keller in the firehouse. In this community room, she and Jonas were alone. "Will you show me the kitchen, Preacher?"

Jonas smiled. She followed him to a doorway in the back of the rental space and into the kitchen. "What do you think?"

Alta looked about the room, noting the small workspace, which would make it difficult for more than two, maybe three, people to prepare breakfast meals. "The kitchen doesn't have much space, but we can make it work if we don't find another one that's more suitable." She took notes and smiled whenever her gaze met Jonas's. "Where to next?"

"The community center," Jonas said. "It's about a quarter mile down the road. I don't know if we have the use of tables and chairs like this fire department allows for us."

Fortunately, the rain held off as Jonas and she headed toward their next stop on their venue tour. It wasn't long until Jonas pulled into the lot then got out and tied up his horse. The building before them looked enormous to Alta.

Jonas observed the woman next to him with a smile as Alta and he entered the New Berne Community Center. Inside they met with the *Englisher*, Mark Decker, who ran it.

"We have several rooms we rent out," Mark said. "From what you've told me about this fundraiser, I suggest this room." He opened a door, revealing a huge room. Much like the room in the firehouse, there were racks of chairs and tables.

"If we decide to hold it, will we be able to use the chairs and tables free of charge?" Alta asked.

"Absolutely," the man assured them.

"May I see the kitchen? We'll need one to prepare the meals."

Smiling at Alta's competency, Jonas waited for Mark to lead the way to the kitchen. He knew for a fact that the kitchen was large enough for several Amish women to cook in. He remained silent as he followed Mark and Alta and was pleased to see Alta's face light up as she stood in the spacious room with the modern gas stove and commercial refrigerator with freezer.

Alta continued to ask Mark questions. Would

our community be able to get into the building early to prepare for the crowd? Mark's answer was yes. How much was the room going to cost? Nothing, Mark said, as the center frequently supported fundraisers that helped the residents of New Berne, and it would be a privilege to do this one for free.

After they finished the tour and gathered the information needed, Jonas helped Alta into his buggy. They pulled out of the parking lot and headed toward the next place on his list.

"Jonas." Alta spoke up when he hadn't gotten that far on the road. "Where are we going next?"

"The VFW." He studied her curiously. "Why?"

She tucked a wayward strand of hair under her *kapp*. "Is it bigger than the community center or firehouse?"

"Nay." Jonas met her gaze.

"I like the community center. It has a large kitchen and plenty of room. Is there any other place like the center or firehouse? Either one of those will work. I don't think we need to pay for a venue, do you?"

His grin reached his eyes. "I agree." He faced the road.

"Which do you prefer?" She could see a lingering upward curve of his lips.

"The community center," he said as he shot her a glance.

Spending time with him made her stomach feel as if it was filled with butterflies. "If there is no need to go anywhere else, what's next?" she asked.

"We eat lunch and make plans," he said right before he turned into the parking lot for Fannie's Luncheonette on the left. After pulling up to the hitching post, he climbed out, tied up his horse then came around to help Alta from the buggy. "You met my *dochter*. This is her place. I think you'll enjoy the food here."

Alta stopped him as he led her to the front entrance door. "I could have made us lunch back at the *haus*," she said, feeling uncomfortable with dining out with him.

"I wanted to take you here. Consider it a thank-you for all the work you're about to do." He smiled at her.

"Jonas—"

He placed a hand on her lower back and pressed her to continue. She jolted at his touch. "Stop overthinking and let us enjoy a nice lunch together," Jonas said. "You brought your pad and pencil, so we can discuss plans for the fundraiser while we eat."

"*Dat*!" Fannie looked pleased when he and Alta entered the restaurant. "Are you here for lunch?"

Jonas flashed Alta a smile. "If you can convince Alta here that it's *oll recht* to eat a meal with me." He heard Alta's gasp before he led her toward his favorite table near the window. He pulled out a chair for her then sat down across from her.

"Do you want a menu?" his daughter asked. "Or do you want me to give you today's special?" Fannie gazed at Alta with warmth. "Do you like stuffed meat loaf?" she asked.

"I've never had it," Alta admitted, blushing. "It sounds delicious."

"It's a favorite of my customers," Fannie said. "There's cheese inside. The dish comes with mashed potatoes and glazed carrots. Is that *okey* with you?"

Jonas saw Alta relax under Fannie's genuine friendliness. "*Ja,* it sounds *wunderbor.*"

His daughter nodded then turned to him. "Fresh iced raisin bread?"

"Always." He studied Alta's pretty features, noting the vivid green of her eyes and the natural arch of her eyebrows, a blond color darker than her hair. He wondered how old she was but refused to ask her directly. *I'll ask Lovina.* Jonas had no idea why it was important, but for some reason, he needed to know how close in age she was to him.

"Iced tea?" Fannie asked.

"Ja, danki," Alta said, looking everywhere but at him.

His daughter left and returned with two tall glasses of iced tea with lemon slices. She placed one in front of each of them before she left.

"So, we've decided to use the community center," Jonas began.

"Ja. The kitchen is perfect for our event."

Jonas enjoyed the sight of her. "We talked earlier about serving breakfast foods for the fundraiser."

Flipping open her pad, she skimmed what she'd written. "Pancakes or waffles served plain or with chocolate chips. We can offer them the choice of fruit toppings such as strawberries and hot apples with or without whipped cream or simply with butter and syrup. Some might prefer eggs and sausage or bacon so I suggest we make different types of breakfast casseroles, which we'll be able to cook or re-heat in an oven."

"I knew you'd be *gut* at this," Jonas said with a grin. He found her ensuing blush endearing.

Fannie brought them her meat loaf special. The aroma alone was mouthwatering to Jonas, who knew how well his youngest daughter could cook. She had opened the restaurant a year ago, and it hadn't taken long for her business to become successful. Everyone enjoyed her food that was available at reasonable prices.

"This smells *wunderbor*, Fannie," Alta praised as Fannie placed a plate in front of her.

His daughter smiled in Alta's direction as she set down his plate. "I hope it tastes as *gut*."

"I know it does," Jonas said as he picked up his fork and cut off a bite-sized piece of meat loaf. Before he put it in his mouth, he observed Alta take a nibble then close her eyes in the enjoyment of the seasonings and cheese that Fannie used to make the meat special.

Alta's appreciation for his daughter's cooking allowed him to delight in her company and Fannie's delicious food. He saw Alta take a forkful of mashed potatoes and place them between her lips. Her expression as she savored the side dish could only be described as one of utter contentment.

"Gut?" he asked.

She blinked as if she'd just realized that he'd been watching her as she ate. Her face turned bright red, and he gave her a soft smile as he buttered the raisin bread that Fannie had brought to accompany the meal.

"It's delicious." Alta took a bite of a glazed carrot. "Where did she learn to cook like this?" Then as if realizing that she might have said something that would bring up painful memories, she looked down at her place and continued to eat as if not expecting an answer.

Jonas softened inside as he watched her. "It wasn't from her mother. My *frau* wasn't a *gut* cook."

Alta's eyes locked with his. "I'm sorry. I didn't mean—"

"You didn't," he assured her. "Fannie has been gifted with the talent for creating new dishes and desserts. She can make all the standard dishes our family always enjoyed." Jonas leaned across the table as if to tell her a secret. "But much better than when... Lena was alive."

She appeared mortified by what she'd stirred up.

"Alta, it's fine. I don't mind sharing with you." He took a drink of iced tea. "Save room for one of Fannie's desserts."

Her green eyes widened. "After eating all this?"

Jonas laughed at the look on her face. "We'll take something to go then," he assured her as he continued to chuckle at her expression.

As they ate, he encouraged Alta to discuss their next steps in getting others within the community on board to help.

"We can start with my *schweschter*." Alta finished her mashed potatoes and then ate more of the carrots. "I'm sure Lovina will help with volunteers. I'm at a disadvantage since I don't know many folks here."

"I'm sure Fannie will want to pitch in." Jonas had finished his meal and pushed his plate to one side.

"Fannie will want to do what?" his daughter asked as she came to check on them.

"Help with the Esh fundraiser. We've decided to do breakfast. Alta suggested we have a bake sale as well so customers can buy delicious desserts to take home with them."

"That's a *wunderbor* idea, Alta!" Fannie exclaimed, and Alta beamed with pleasure. "I'll be happy to help with both. I'll close the restaurant for the day and put a sign on the door, suggesting that everyone attend the fundraiser."

Alta looked thrilled. "That's so kind of you."

Jonas found himself drawn to the genuine and sweet woman with a lovely heart. Observing her with interest, he watched Alta jot some notes on her pad. then glance out the window with a smile. The day had cleared and the sun had come out. Suddenly, her smile disappeared and she turned pale.

"I…can we leave?"

"Alta, what's wrong?" Jonas wondered what she'd seen that made her look afraid.

"I must go home. I'm not feeling well," she whispered.

He was deeply concerned when she stood and hugged herself. "I hope it wasn't the food," he said.

"Nay," she gasped. "Headache." But the tell-tale flush of her cheeks said that she wasn't bothered by a headache at all. Something or someone outside had disturbed her enough to make her want to leave.

"Oll recht," he soothed. "Let's go."

Her green eyes flickered with gratitude as he stood and escorted her through the back of the store. For some reason, he knew instinctively that she would have refused to exit through the front entrance.

Jonas could feel her tension as he stopped briefly to pay his daughter for the meal. Fannie argued with him about taking the money, but he pulled rank as her father and made her take it.

His attention back on Alta who waited nervously near the back door, he quickly took her outside and helped her inside the buggy. He climbed in and was ready to leave when Fannie came running out the door with Alta's pad and pencil. Alta accepted it without a word and then seemed to withdraw into herself as he steered his horse back to her sister's.

It was only after he had driven down the road for some time that he could feel the woman beside him relax. She still hadn't said a word, and he didn't want to force her. Jonas wanted to win her trust, and if he pushed too hard, he felt certain he would lose any progress he'd made with her.

He pulled onto the dirt lane that led to Adam and Lovina's home. After parking his buggy, he started to go around to help her out.

"I can get out on my own, Jonas," Alta said, stopping him. She managed to give him a genuine smile. "*Danki.* I enjoyed myself today and look forward to helping with the fundraiser."

"I had a *gut* time, too, Alta," he murmured. "I'll see you on Sunday." He saw her nod then watched as she entered the house.

Jonas was upset. *I will find out who hurt her and why.* For he realized then that something bad must have happened to make her skittish and afraid. And with God's grace and help, he'd discover what, so he could help the woman whose company he'd enjoyed more than any other in a long, long time.

Chapter Six

"Alta." Her sister greeted her with a smile when she looked up from her vegetable garden and saw Alta enter the backyard. "How was your day with Jonas? Did you decide on a place for the fundraiser?"

Alta smiled. "*Ja.* We chose the community center and then we talked about what to serve while we ate lunch at Fannie's Luncheonette."

Lovina arched an eyebrow. "You had lunch together."

"*Ja.*" Alta recalled the wonderful food that Jonas's daughter had prepared for them. "The meal was delicious. Fannie is an incredible cook. We had stuffed meat loaf, mashed potatoes and glazed carrots." She didn't tell Lovina that she'd seen a familiar someone through the front window that had startled her. And made her worry.

"Everyone loves to eat there. I never had her stuffed meat loaf, but I imagine it's tasty."

Alta nodded. "*Ja.* I was too full for dessert." She approached where Lovina was bent over her garden, picking the last of the vegetables to pickle for chow-chow. The back window was open, and she detected the tantalizing scent of cooked apples. "You made an apple pie?"

"*Ja,* I used *Mam*'s recipe," Lovina said.

Fortunately, their *dat* had been a kind man. Even in his grief over his wife's death, he'd been there for Lovina and Alta. He passed away right before Alta turned twenty and her sister's eighteenth birthday. Their *mam* had been a fantastic cook, and everyone in the family and community had benefited from her culinary skills.

It was two in the afternoon. Alta had been gone for over four hours. She knelt by her sister's side. "Can I help?"

"No need but I appreciate the offer. I just finished," Lovina said, as she gestured toward the basket of newly harvested fresh vegetables. "But I could use your help in the kitchen."

"I'll carry these in for you." Alta picked up the basket and stood. She followed her sister into the house and set the basket on the kitchen table.

Lovina tied a quilted apron around her waist and handed one to Alta.

"Isaiah told me he liked my cupcakes this morning," Alta said as she slipped on the apron, ready to work.

"He certainly does enjoy them. He would have eaten all of them if I hadn't stopped him. He isn't the only one who appreciates fine cupcakes." Lovina leaned her back against the counter. "So, what do you need me to do for the fundraiser?"

"I don't know many people here in New Berne. Can you help coordinate volunteers? Those who cook well and those who are better at serving and cleaning tables." Alta watched her sister grab the kettle and put it on the stove to boil.

"Tea?" her sister asked as she took two cups from a top cabinet.

"*Ja,* I'd love some." Alta enjoyed spending time with Lovina. There were no hurt feelings left between them, and she felt grateful for her sister who had opened her home to her and wanted her to stay for an extended visit. She prayed that once Lovina learned the reason she'd left Happiness her sister wouldn't think badly of her.

Lovina poured hot water into the teacups and left the room. When a knock resounded on the back door, she called from the pantry, "Would you mind getting that, Alta?"

"*Ja.*" Alta answered the door, stunned to see who stood on the stoop. "Jonas!" She stepped away to allow him entry. "Did I forget something?"

He took off his hat before he stepped inside, cradling it under his left arm. In his right hand, he carried a paper bag.

"*Nay,*" he said, his deep voice vibrating down her spine. "I did." He handed her the bag.

"What's this?"

"Your dessert from Fannie's. I put it on the back seat and forgot about it until I was almost home." He eyed her carefully. "Are you *oll recht*?" he whispered.

"*Ja.*" Cheeks turning pink, she averted her gaze. The last thing she wanted was for Jonas to ask why she'd wanted to flee the restaurant.

"You know you can talk to me about anything," he murmured.

Alta blinked. "*Danki.*" She couldn't tell him why she was upset. He would think less of her if he knew.

Lovina entered the kitchen and grinned. "Jonas! I didn't expect to see you again today."

"Fannie gave Alta and me some dessert to take with us, and I forgot to give your sister hers."

"What is it?" Alta asked him.

"Lemon squares and chocolate brownies. I hope you like at least one of those."

Alta looked surprised. "I like both. But what about you? Which do you like better? You should keep whatever you enjoy."

"Those are for you." Jonas's lips curved. "Fannie keeps me in desserts. You don't have to worry about that. She gave me the same ones." His eyes on her, he seemed to hesitate. "I should go. I have things to do before Fannie gets home."

"Will you come for Visiting Day?" Lovina asked. "I thought I'd ask several families with women I know who would be happy to help with organizing volunteers for the fundraiser."

"I'd like that." Jonas fiddled with his hat in his hands. "Alta, *danki* for your help today."

"You're *willkomm*, Jonas." She smiled. She'd enjoyed the day. "I appreciate the desserts. Please let Fannie know."

Jonas nodded. "I'll see you on Sunday." He settled his hat on his head and left.

Alta experienced the sudden loss of his presence, which startled her. Jonas made her feel safe and happy. She looked forward to working with him on the fundraiser. Watching him leave from the window, Alta found herself smiling as she returned his wave.

"Jonas is a handsome man, *ja*?" Lovina said with a smirk as Alta turned from the window.

Alta blushed. "I... I suppose so."

Her sister shut off the flame under the kettle. "Shall we have tea and enjoy Fannie's desserts?"

"*Ja,* sounds *gut*," Alta said, glad Lovina had dropped the subject of Jonas Miller. Despite the disturbing yet familiar sight of the man she'd seen through the front window earlier at Fannie's restaurant, Alta experienced a renewed sense of hope.

Throughout the day on Friday, Alta worked beside her sister to get ready for Visiting Day on Sunday. Lovina and Adam had invited more families than usual. These members of the New Berne Amish community would be instrumental in holding a successful fundraiser for the Esh family. Lovina, Alta and her nieces—Lovina's daughters—cleaned the house from top to bottom in preparation for Sunday's gathering. On Saturday morning, Alta was in the kitchen with her sister baking and cooking up a storm to make sure there was plenty of food for everyone who attended. By late evening, Alta saw that everything was ready for their visitors and she went to bed, satisfied with all they had accomplished.

Sunday morning the family was up early, excited to see family and friends who would arrive midmorning.

The first ones to visit were Gabriel and Lucy Fisher with their children.

"Lucy Fisher is a master baker," her sister said, after introducing the couple to Alta. "She sells her baked goods out of their family store. Gabriel makes toys and other wooden objects which he has for sale."

"A master baker," Alta murmured with a smile for the pretty young woman, who was a mother of three. "I'll have to stop in and buy something."

"No need," Lucy replied, beaming. "I'll be happy to give you samples of my baked goods." She leaned close to Alta and whispered as if what she said was a secret. "I brought two cakes and a pie."

Alta grinned. "What kind?"

"Chocolate cake with fudge frosting and cherry cake with vanilla frosting. The pie is a mixed berry."

"They sound delicious!"

Another couple approached with their children. The wife was pregnant. The husband was tall, good-looking and he seemed to have eyes only for the lovely woman by his side.

"Micah and Katie Bontrager," Lovina said

with a look of delight to see the family of five. "This is Alta, my *schweschter*."

"*Hallo,*" Alta greeted. "It's nice to meet you." She smiled as she watched a little boy cling to his mother's skirts while Micah carried his two little girls. "Are you a baker, too, Katie?"

The young woman with blond hair and blue eyes nodded. "I bake, *ja*, but my specialty is breakfast." She exchanged loving glances with her husband. "Especially breakfast casseroles."

"That's *wunderbor*!" Alta exclaimed, pleased to hear it. "I enjoy breakfast casseroles, too."

"There is something special about Katie's," her husband said. "She makes several kinds."

Katie grinned. "And I'll be happy to make them for the Esh fundraiser."

"*Danki!*" Alta was pleased. She could already envision how well the event would go. "Jonas is going to reach out to schedule a date at the community center. I'll let you know once we have one."

Everyone had gone into the house, leaving her and Jonas alone.

"I thought we could have it a week from next Saturday," Jonas said. He stepped closer to her. "Is that doable?" he murmured.

Alta nodded, aware of how attractive he was. "I don't see why not."

"There are some event details we'll need to

discuss," he told her softly. "Are you available on Tuesday?"

"*Ja,* what time?" Alta looked forward to the outing. She had enjoyed spending time in Jonas's company, working with him to help a family who desperately needed financial help.

"Ten again?" His warm brown gaze seemed to see right through her.

"That will be fine." She hoped she was mistaken and he couldn't see what she'd been trying so hard to hide, because the last thing she wanted was for him to know she saw her son-in-law Ethan outside of Fannie's and feared he would humiliate her by telling her off publicly for nattering about her daughter's miscarriage.

She and Jonas entered the house to join the others and became separated as friends took up his attention while Lovina grabbed her to introduce her to different people. The women she met offered to cook for the fundraiser, and their husbands volunteered to set up tables and chairs as well as be available to help wherever needed. Alta was startled to find her thoughts frequently centered on the kind, handsome minister. Her eyes were drawn to him as he chatted with his friends and neighbors in her brother-in-law and sister's great room.

Jonas Miller was a wildly handsome man with an endearing charm, and it was hard for her to ignore that. Because he was a preacher and a church elder, she mustn't allow herself to think about him as anything other than someone with whom she was working on the fundraiser. The way she'd lived her life for years now had hurt others, and she knew Jonas would see what a terrible person she was if he ever found out. But she couldn't help but throw caution aside whenever he was within distance because she trusted him and was sure he'd never find out unless she told him, which she didn't plan to do.

By the time families had left for home, Alta dropped, exhausted, onto the sofa in her sister's great room. Jonas stayed behind, and butterflies in her stomach fought her attraction whenever he was near. She thought of all the work they needed to do together to make sure the fundraiser was successful.

"It was a great day." Jonas sat next to her.

"It was," Alta admitted, with satisfaction and something else—something she seemed to feel whenever Jonas was nearby.

"I was wondering if you would like to go with me to the community center tomorrow afternoon rather than Tuesday morning?" he asked. "I have a few things to do in the morning, but I'll be free later in the day."

Although everything inside of her warned

her to keep an emotional distance from Jonas, Alta knew she couldn't stay away. "I'd like that. What time did you have in mind?"

"Two?" He looked hopeful.

"Should I meet you there—at the center?" Alta waited to hear what he had to say. She knew the community center was in the opposite direction from Lovina's house and closer to his.

Jonas frowned as if the thought of her traveling by herself bothered him. "*Nay*, I'll be here at two."

She nodded, pleased with his answer, although she shouldn't be.

His daughter Fannie entered the room, her eyes brightening when she saw her father. "I'm ready to leave whenever you are, *Dat*."

"I'm ready." To Alta's disappointment, Jonas stood. "I'll see you tomorrow, Alta."

"Have a *gut* night, Jonas." She rose and followed the two toward the back door, the closest entrance to her brother-in-law's dirt driveway. When Jonas turned and grinned at her once he'd stepped out, her heart and spirits lightened until she reminded herself that a relationship with a man, especially a minister, could never be.

The morning of the fundraiser had arrived. Jonas, assisted by the men within the community, set up tables and chairs in the massive room at the New Berne Community Center. He was pleased with the preparations for the event. He and Alta had secured this date, November 12, and everything regarding the fundraiser had fallen into place.

Alta had made signs to place in local businesses. Her talent for making them had surprised and pleased him. She had handed them out at church Sunday and had given some to the members of his Amish sect to deliver them to places she might have forgotten. Preacher David Bontrager had also announced details for the event after service.

Lovina and her family weren't there yet. Jonas had hoped Alta would arrive earlier, but he understood that she'd go with her sister for a ride. He should have offered to bring her, but he didn't want to make her uncomfortable since Lovina was coming to help, and it might seem strange if Alta had come to the center with him. Also, he had Fannie and all the wonderful dishes she'd made and baked, which filled the entire back bench seat of his buggy. He had picked up his daughter early this morning from her luncheonette to help her transport everything she was donating to the cause.

It had been a pleasure to work with Alta. She had accompanied him as they finalized the venue's arrangements. Afterward, they'd discussed a few other items rather than getting it done later in the week.

And now the day was here. As he worked, Jonas found himself glancing at the door frequently with the hope of seeing Alta's arrival. When an hour went by and the Kings and Alta hadn't shown, he grew worried. Had something happened to one of them? Or to Alta?

Suddenly, the door opened and Alta rushed in, followed by the King family.

"I'm sorry I'm late! My nephew fell and hurt himself. We wanted to make sure he was *oll recht* before we left!" Alta appeared distraught, as if she'd done something wrong, which she hadn't. She was carrying a large box of what he saw were cupcakes.

Jonas couldn't help smiling at her. "You're fine. The fundraiser doesn't start until nine." He checked his watch. "It's only eight fifteen." He headed to the kitchen with her closely following. When they entered the kitchen, he grinned as he showed her the various desserts lined up on a stainless steel counter on the far side of the room. To his surprise when he faced her, Alta appeared embarrassed. "Alta?"

She blinked and dropped her head. "I only brought cupcakes, nothing as *gut* as those."

He bent low so she would have to meet his

eyes. "I've had your cupcakes. They are delicious! Why are you so worried?"

Alta shrugged. "I wasn't a *gut* baker. I only learned to do better over the years."

"Everything we do is a learning experience," he said as he took the cupcakes from her and set them with the other desserts.

Lovina burst into the kitchen with a large pan in her arms. "Your breakfast casserole," she said as she smiled at her sister. She set a baking dish down and left as quickly as she'd come.

"You made a breakfast casserole, too?" As she gave a nod, he couldn't help but wonder why Alta thought she wasn't giving enough for this event. She'd planned it with him, and she'd made a dessert and something to heat up and serve for breakfast. "Alta, you've given more to help than anyone else. Because of you, I know our fundraiser will be a success."

Jonas watched her face brighten.

"Danki," she murmured.

He shook his head as he retrieved the breakfast casserole and placed it on the counter in a different, empty space. "No need to thank me, Alta. I should be the one saying it to you." Jonas enjoyed this woman, and he hated that she suffered from self-doubt. Jonas wondered again what had happened to her. Alta wasn't a child, and he thought how it was unusual for someone her age to be dealing with a lack of confidence.

As Jonas struggled with what he could do to help, three women entered the kitchen, stopping him from questioning Alta, who had been reluctant thus far to confide in him about her past and her presence in her sister's home. A sister from whom until recently she'd been estranged.

Lucy Fisher came into the room with her husband Gabriel bringing in more desserts and another casserole.

Alta seemed to forget her inner troubles as soon as she saw the younger couple. "Lucy, you've outdone yourself. *Danki*! Your contribution is bound to make our fundraiser successful."

Lucy smiled. "I know what it's like to need help from our community. I'm always willing to give back to our church family who has been *wunderbor* to me and Gabriel."

After the Fishers left, Jonas checked his wristwatch and saw that it was time to turn on the oven to reheat the casseroles. "What temperature will we need?" he said, gesturing toward the large oven. It was a cook's dream with two separate compartments and heat settings. He was familiar with this type of appliance since Fannie had purchased one for her restaurant before she'd opened the place for business.

"I'd set the top oven at three hundred fifty and the bottom at four hundred." She wore a frown after he'd set the temperatures and faced her.

"Alta?" Jonas pondered about her thoughts. "What's wrong?"

She managed a smile, but he saw through it to catch a glimpse of her vulnerability. After a long hesitation, she answered. "I—ah—do we have a table set up for the bake sale?"

"*Ja.* And I've got the fixings for the pancakes and waffles. Fannie brought fruit toppings and syrup for both."

Alta furrowed her brow. "I know I suggested waffles, but how are we going to make them?"

Pulling two waffle makers from a cabinet, Jonas grinned. "The center has these we can use. This isn't the first time this type of fundraiser has been held here."

She looked relieved. "Praise to the Lord." Alta searched the room. "Who is bringing the eggs?"

"Like these?" Lovina said as she entered with a box full of filled egg cartons.

"Lovina, that is your livelihood," Alta said with concern.

"These aren't all ours. Adam just got here after buying what he could at the grocery store."

"*Danki, schweschter.*" Alta helped her sister find a space for the eggs.

Jonas watched the exchange between the two sisters. He saw how Alta's face softened whenever she talked with Lovina. There was love and gratitude in Alta's green eyes as the women chatted about the best way to organize the kitchen and who would cook and who would serve their "guests."

"Jonas, we can use your help," Lovina's husband said from the open doorway to the dining area.

With a nod in his direction, Jonas addressed Alta and her sister. "If there is anything else you need, please let me know, and I'll make sure you get it."

Then Jonas left the kitchen with the mental image of Alta's sweet expression as she listened to his last words. And an ache settled in his chest with the desire to learn more about Alta Hershberger and how he might help her once he knew her secrets.

Chapter Seven

Alta stood near the door of the community center to greet their customers before she showed them to a table. People stopping briefly to check out the desserts on the way in and then buy a sweet after they'd enjoyed their meal satisfied her.

"Alta, where would you like me to put this?" Katie Bontrager held up a baking pan as she approached. "Aaron Hostetler just dropped it off. He said it was from his neighbor, the Widow Troyer, who was unable to attend but still wanted to contribute to the cause."

Bending to peek, Alta recognized a casserole made of hashed-brown potatoes and cheese. "Looks delicious. Do me a favor and give it to Lovina. Tell her to go ahead and put it in the oven to warm." Her sister had agreed to oversee the work in the kitchen to make sure the food was ready to be served to anyone who came in to eat. The tables were full, and as the diners left, others were there to take their place.

Since nine in the morning, Alta had been continually checking to see who needed help, and she was quick to fulfill orders when everyone else was too busy with other customers.

Near the end of the event, her niece Esther approached with a furrowed brow. "*Endie* Alta, the man over at that table," she said, gesturing toward one part of the room, "is unhappy because there is no coffee left."

There were three thirty-cup coffeemakers set out in the dining room. Each pot had been utilized differently. One held regular coffee, the second one decaf while a third was filled with hot water for tea and hot chocolate mix.

"I'll talk with him," Alta said with an encouraging smile for her niece. "Don't let him upset you. You've done a *wunderbor* job today. *Danki* for your hard work."

Esther grinned. *"Danki."*

As she approached the man's table, Alta greeted him with a smile. "I'm happy that you've come to eat with us. Is there something I can get for you?"

The English customer looked as if he were in his mid-to-late thirties. "There's no coffee," he said irritably. "I need coffee to drink with my meal."

"I apologize. I made a small pot in the back in case we ran out in here. May I bring you a cup?"

The man gave her a genuine smile. "Thank you. That would be great."

"My pleasure." Alta glanced at the others at the table. "Would anyone else like coffee?"

"No, the rest of us have something to drink, but thanks for asking," a woman replied. She looked to be the same age as the man.

Probably his wife since he has her and two young kids at the same table. Alta smiled at the man. "I'll get you that coffee. Thank you for your patience and understanding."

She unplugged the empty pot and then entered the kitchen toward the smaller drip coffeemaker she'd turned on earlier. "The large pot of regular is finished. I'm going to grab a cup from here to serve." She poured a large mugful.

Lovina smiled. "That was *gut* thinking, *schweschter*, when you decided to make more in here."

Alta grinned at her sister before she headed back to the dining room. "Here you are," she told the man back at the table. "I forgot to ask what you took in it so I brought these." Alta placed an assortment of sweeteners and a bowl with small containers of half-and-half.

"Thank you." The man tipped his head in

appreciation. "And the food is delicious. If you ever have another fundraiser, we'll be there. We couldn't make it sooner this morning."

"Where did you hear about it?" Alta asked.

He added a spoonful of sugar to his cup. "We saw a sign at the hardware store."

Alta smiled. She was glad that their home-made signs had worked to keep the tables filled with customers. After hearing compliments on their meal choices, she knew everything was going according to plan.

At one forty-five in the afternoon, Alta decided not to allow anyone else to be seated, but she offered to fix the late newcomers' plates to go, which made more than one family happy.

Soon, it was two fifteen, and the fundraiser was over. The women worked to clean up tables and, in the kitchen, while the men put away the cleared tables and chairs. Alta helped in the dining room then went into the kitchen to see what she could do to contribute. But the kitchen workers had put everything away. Dishes were in the dishwasher, which had been turned on. All the desserts on the bake table had been purchased, which made her realize that holding a bake sale in conjunction with the breakfast had paid off. She was eager to discover how much the fundraiser made.

"Brrr," Katie said as she reentered the build-

ing to get the last of her dishes. "The temperature outside has dropped considerably, and the sky is getting dark. Be safe going home."

Alta nodded. "We'll be careful. You stay safe, too, Katie. And *danki* for everything."

"I was happy to help," the young woman said before she left.

All the volunteers departed, except for Jonas and her. Alone with him, Alta was extremely conscious of his presence…his good looks. The way his dark hair shone under the overhead light. He wore a royal blue shirt with black pants and suspenders. His warm brown eyes were soft as he waved toward a small table for two in the corner of the rented room.

"Let's see how much we made," Jonas said as he placed the metal money box down. He opened it and handed Alta a stack of paper money, then set the small change in the center of the table. "Why don't we make stacks of each denomination?"

"Okey." Alta smiled as she started to count bills. "It looks like we did well."

"Ja. Let's see how much we made." Jonas grinned at her, and the little laugh lines at the outer corners of his eyes gave him character, making him more strikingly handsome to her.

Forty-five minutes later, they had counted the money, walked through the rented space to make sure everything was in order and met Frank Hadden, who had arranged the room for them. Frank was satisfied with how clean everything was after the fundraiser. Jonas thanked him, and then he led Alta out of the building.

"It's sleeting!" Alta gasped. She saw that ice mixed with snow covered the landscape and street.

Gazing up at the dark sky, Jonas frowned. If the sleet continued, the road would become treacherous for buggies and cars. "We can't stay here," he said gently, wishing they could wait it out. "I'm not sure how far we'll get in this mess. We'll see how we make out." He thought he could make it home if not to the Kings' residence.

"Be careful." He reached for her arm to steady her when she started to slip.

"Danki," Alta whispered, looking terrified as their gazes met.

"Alta, I won't let anything happen to you." His lips curved upward as he held onto her arm. "I'll keep you safe."

He could feel her tense up as he helped her into his buggy before he skirted the vehicle to unhitch his horse from a wooden post and then climb inside. Once seated, he gently settled his fingers over her hand that gripped the bench seat with white-knuckled fingers. At his touch, she looked at him with fear in her green eyes and a quivering mouth. Jonas gave her a confident smile he hoped would comfort her.

With a light flick of the leathers, he steered the horse-drawn buggy out of the parking lot and onto the road in the direction of his house. Jonas heard Alta inhale sharply and saw that she continued to grip the bench seat, her knuckles white. He needed to find a way to distract her. Something about her anxiety made him worry and wonder. Had she once been in a buggy accident?

"We made $4,500," he said cheerfully, hoping to win her attention. "And that's just on breakfast. I'm amazed that the bake sale brought in over $500." He smiled at her when he saw he had her attention. "You did *gut*, Alta."

Alta gave him a small smile. "*We* did, Jonas. Many volunteered and donated food. It's *wunderbor* how everyone stepped in to help one way or another."

Jonas was grateful to see her relax a bit. "We may need another fundraiser, but the money raised today is a fine start in helping the Esh family. It's hard enough when a child needs surgery but then for the *eldra* to worry about paying the bill…"

"Is terrible," Alta finished. "We are fortunate

that our Amish communities work together to help families in need."

A car zoomed up from behind, skidding a bit as it continued past. Jonas felt Alta tense up as she stared at the vehicle's taillights. He wanted to ask if she'd ever been in a buggy accident but he stayed silent.

"The sleet is falling harder," Alta said. "I can hear the ice on top of your buggy."

In reply, Jonas turned on the blinker and into his dairy farm. "Here we are—safe!" He smiled at her.

She appeared surprised and relieved. "Where are we?"

"My *haus*," he said. "We'll stay here to see if the weather improves. Fannie is home. She can make us something to eat while we wait for the storm to pass. *Ja*?" He saw her nod. "Stay in the buggy until I come around to help you." He got out then slid open a barn door and brought his mare inside. Once the animal was in her stable, Jonas returned for Alta.

"Careful," he warned as he reached up to help her. She nodded as she held onto his hand and stepped down onto the ice-covered driveway.

"She doesn't have to go to any trouble," she said.

Jonas helped her negotiate the icy steps. "She loves to cook. Remember she owns a restaurant." He opened the side door. "Fannie! I'm home, and we have company!" After taking her coat to hang up, he seated her at the kitchen table and put on the teakettle. "Fannie!"

"Coming, *Dat*!" his daughter called down from upstairs. She entered the room a few moments later. "Alta! *Hallo!* I'm glad you're here."

Jonas enjoyed the blush on Alta's cheeks and the glimmer of delight in her pretty green eyes. Her royal blue dress was lovely, worn with a full-length black apron. She wore a white organza *kapp* over her golden blond hair.

"*Danki,* Fannie," Alta replied.

"Are you hungry?" Fannie asked. "Alta, I didn't see you stop to eat once during the fundraiser."

"I didn't." Alta played with one of her *kapp* strings. "I was too busy to eat."

Jonas eyed Alta with concern. "We're hungry. Would you mind fixing us something?"

Alta shook her head. "Please don't go to any bother."

"It's no bother at all," his daughter assured Alta. She turned to him. "*Dat*, what do you feel like eating?"

"Whatever you make will be fine." Jonas gazed at his daughter, happy with her kind and generous nature. Someday, he knew, Fannie would marry, leaving him alone in the house for the first time. The thought saddened him, but he wanted her to be happy.

"Here," Fannie said with a smile after fixing them tea. "Why don't you go into the great room and enjoy your tea while I cook?"

"I'd like to help." Alta looked worried. "You shouldn't have to do all the work."

"I have a macaroni and cheese casserole already made. I'll just pop it into the oven. It won't take long." Fannie took a baking dish out of the refrigerator and set it on the kitchen counter. "Do you like macaroni and cheese?" she asked Alta.

"Ja." Alta's face lit up with a genuine smile. "I love it, but I can't recall the last time I've had it."

"Fannie's is *wunderbar*," Jonas said. "Let's do what my *dochter* has requested and head into the great room. We have a great view of our backyard there."

After pushing the sheer curtains open, Jonas maneuvered two chairs to face the large double window. He set a small table between them for their teacups. The sleet had turned mostly to snow, he noticed. After witnessing Alta's fear during the ride, he wondered how she'd feel about heading toward her sister's if the weather didn't let up before dark.

"This is a lovely view." Alta walked closer to the window and peered outside. "The sleet has changed to snow," she gasped before she took a seat. "The roads…"

Jonas studied her with concern. "I won't take the buggy out if the streets are bad."

Closing her eyes, Alta released a sharp breath before she looked across the table at him. "My husband was killed on a snowy day. A car slid into the back of his buggy and…"

He reached across the table to gently capture her hand. "I'm sorry. I thought you seemed…"

"Scared?" she said with a nod. "*Ja,* I have a hard time whenever I travel in sleet or snow. Sleet and ice are the worst." She glanced away. "You must think me a foolish woman."

"*Nay,*" Jonas said with conviction as he gave her hand a little squeeze. "We all have things we're afraid of. You have *gut* reason to be fearful of winter weather."

Alta's eyes glistened with tears. "It was so long ago. I should be over it by now."

"Some things aren't easy to get over," he whispered, moved by her sadness, her worry. "Does Lovina have a cell phone?" Jonas refused to put her through the ordeal of taking her home in bad weather.

She shook her head. "I don't think so, although one of my nieces might have one."

"If you need to stay, we'll find a way to reach them," he reassured her.

Stunned, Alta could only stare at him. "Spend the night? I don't know…"

"You can stay with Fannie…"

"Did I hear my name?" his daughter asked as she entered the room.

Jonas returned her smile as he picked up his teacup. "I suggested that Alta stay here until morning if road conditions don't improve. I assured her you wouldn't mind sharing."

Fannie grinned. "I will be happy to share my room with you, Alta. My *schweschter* used to share with me, but Sadie has married and no longer lives at home." She cradled her cup then took a sip, swallowed. "There are two beds," she added.

"*Dochter,* did you bring your cell phone home from the restaurant?" Jonas felt grateful when Fannie nodded. "If we can't travel because of the weather, we need to let Lovina know where Alta is and that I'll bring her back as soon as it's safe."

Fannie nodded. "I'll call her niece," she said. "I have her number. Esther is permitted to have a phone because of her cleaning business." She took another drink of tea. "The casserole will be ready soon. I'll call you after I take it out of the oven."

"Did you want me to set the table?" Alta asked.

Fannie gazed at her with a soft expression. *"Danki,* but it's already done." She left, leaving Jonas alone with Alta again.

He studied the woman by his side. "What's wrong?"

Alta appeared worried. "I don't know about staying here, Jonas. What will everyone think?"

"You forget I'm a minister. They will think nothing of us staying safely off the road until the snow and ice are cleared."

"I hope you're right," she said, clearly not appeased.

"Dat!" Fannie called from the other room. "Time to eat!"

Jonas rose, took Alta's cup from her then nodded for her to precede him. "Please don't worry, Alta," he said quietly. "I won't allow anyone to malign you. You have worked hard for this community today. Everyone looked to you for directions. You are a *gut* woman. Believe me when I say everything will be fine."

He eyed her thoughtfully as he walked behind her, noticing the slump in her shoulders. Jonas needed to know what made Alta concern herself about how others regarded her. Maybe this evening he'd learn more about the woman who intrigued him like no other. A woman he was starting to have feelings for.

Chapter Eight

"This casserole is delicious, Fannie," Alta praised with a smile. "I've never had any this *gut*."

Fannie beamed at her. "It was my *mam's* recipe." Her smile fell as she looked at her father. "*Dat*, I miss her."

Jonas nodded. "We all do."

Alta saw the sadness in his brown gaze. She understood how he felt, having lost her husband at an early age. "Your *mam* must have been a *wunderbor* cook," she said softly.

"Fannie is better," Jonas replied. His regard for his daughter held affection.

"*Dat*—"

"It's *oll recht, dochter*." His smile for her was filled with warmth.

Something shifted inside of Alta, a tug of emotion that made her like Jonas even more than previously. He truly was a fine human being who cared about others, a man with a past that hadn't defined him, making him worthy in the eyes of God. While she… Alta blinked and wished that she was worthy of Jonas.

"You're not eating," Jonas pointed out with a look toward her plate where she'd been playing with her food. "I thought you liked it."

"I do." Alta picked up her fork and began eating again. The dish was more than delicious, but she'd been temporarily lost in thought. "I'm afraid I was thinking about something."

"Care to share?" Jonas gazed at her with an intensity that shook her while it drew her in. His expression was warm, his mouth forming an upward curve.

"*Nay,* but *danki.* It wasn't anything important." Alta glanced out the window to see the snow falling, although it had lessened in strength. "Looks like the weather may be improving soon."

"*Ja,* but it's still freezing outside, which means the roads are still covered with ice and snow." He studied her with concern. "Are you worried about being here? With us?"

Was she? She was in danger of liking Jonas too much, and while she knew she should avoid him, she enjoyed time in his company too much to stay away.

"*Nay,* I'm not concerned," she admitted. "As long as Lovina doesn't worry about me."

"She won't," Fannie said. "Esther said she would explain the situation. I'm sure your *schweschter* would rather you spend the night here with us than be out traveling on icy streets."

"You're *recht,*" Alta admitted as she transferred her attention to the man seated at the table. That brief look was telling, as Jonas seemed relieved to hear that she didn't mind sleeping over in his daughter's room.

It was getting dark out. The snow continued to fall. The wind had picked up, making visibility too difficult to travel. She felt suddenly nervous. It was awkward, for she had no belongings with her. What would she sleep in? What time did the two go to bed? Alta decided to take her cues from Fannie since she would be staying with her.

They finished their supper, and Fannie brought out a pie from a back room. "Chocolate peanut butter," she said as she set it down with a flourish. "I hope you don't mind, *Dat,* but I kept this one for us."

Jonas laughed, the rich sound rippling down Alta's spine. "My favorite. *Danki.* It would have been hard to see it for sale on the bake table."

"It looks…" After seeing Jonas's expression and hearing his joy, Alta was at a loss for words.

"You're not allergic to peanuts, are you?" Fannie said worriedly.

Alta shook her head. *"Nay."*

The younger woman grinned. *"Gut!"* She grabbed a knife and then took plates out of the cabinet and set them next to the pie. "How big of a piece would you like, *Dat*?"

"Half the pie?" he said with a teasing twinkle in his brown eyes.

"Wait!" Alta exclaimed, drawing his attention. "If you eat half the pie, would there be any left for you to eat tomorrow?" When Jonas frowned, she added, "I want at least a quarter piece and I'm sure Fannie does, too." Glancing at Fannie, she was pleased to see her nod vigorously, playing along with her.

"Fine," Jonas said with a fake huff. "I'll take whatever you give me." But his grin was wide and his eyes were merry.

Alta couldn't control her laughter. "Poor *boo*," she said cheekily. "I'm sure you'll go hungry with the slice that Fannie is about to cut for you."

Jonas stared at her for a long minute, and she felt self-conscious until she saw his expression soften as if he was pleased with her good humor and ability to poke fun at him. He turned toward his daughter. "Fannie, give her half the pie," he uttered seriously.

"Nay!" Alta gasped. "I couldn't possibly eat that much!"

Jonas grinned. "Have you ever had a chocolate peanut butter pie like this, Alta?"

She shook her head. "Never."

"Then you're in for a treat!" Jonas exchanged looks with his daughter, who nodded. "If you don't like it, I'll eat it for you."

Alta arched an eyebrow. *"Nay*, preacher. I'll bring it home for my *schweschter* to try!" She cracked up when she saw his expression.

Seeing the humor in the situation, Fannie joined in. "She's told you, *Vadder*!"

Gazing at the pie, Alta detected the delicious scent and was eager for a taste. She scooped a sample up and placed it between her lips using a fork. The wonderful smooth texture and mouthwatering flavors sat on her tongue, providing her pleasure before she swallowed it. Feeling the focus of two sets of eyes, she looked over and saw Fannie and Jonas waiting to see how she liked it.

"I'm sorry, Jonas. Fannie, but I'll not be sharing this pie with anyone. It's delicious!" Alta grinned. "Do you sell these in your restaurant?"

"On occasion. Most of the time, I prefer to

make it for our family," Fannie admitted with an embarrassed smile.

"Then I'm honored you allowed me to have some," Alta said sincerely. *"Danki."*

"You're most *willkomm*," Fannie said as her father nodded in agreement.

Jonas observed Alta as she enjoyed her pie. She wore a smile that made him feel warm and happy inside. He could tell she'd been nervous when the topic came up for her to spend the night, but the roads were terrible, and he realized that she was deathly afraid of him driving over the snow and ice. It felt strange having another woman in the house other than his daughter. There had been no one here since Lena had passed, and although the church elders had been pressuring him to remarry, he'd been unable to even think of replacing his beloved wife.

He didn't know what he'd have done if Fannie hadn't been here. It would have been wrong if Alta had stayed alone with him, but Jonas knew that his daughter would make Alta feel welcomed and safe.

Jonas never expected to be put in this position, to have a woman overnight at his house. To make matters more uncomfortable for him, his feelings for Alta were complicated and unexpected. The woman had something bothering her. Whether it was from her past or present, he had no idea. And he knew she would be leaving sometime soon. But he could only hope that she'd stay. He liked her. A lot.

He could hear Fannie and Alta talking, saw Alta lick some chocolate off her bottom lip. They were like young girls, at ease with each other, and Jonas thanked the Lord that Fannie was here for however long he would have her at home.

Alta got up from her seat and moved to peer out the window. The town had put a streetlight in front of his house, and there was enough glow on his property to see the weather. "It hasn't eased up," she said with a furrow between her brows as she turned to glance from him to Fannie.

"All the more reason to spend the night," Jonas said and was glad to see Fannie bob her head in agreement. "How about we go into the great room for a while before we head upstairs?"

Fannie had turned on a battery-operated LED lantern which she placed toward the back of the table. The play of light on Alta's face had him eyeing her more than he should. "Sounds nice," his daughter said. "Or do you want to play Dutch Blitz right here?"

"Do you know to play?" he asked Alta.

"*Ja.* It was a favorite of J…" Her voice tapered off and her face sobered. "We played it often when my girls were little."

"What would you prefer, the game or to read in the other room?" Jonas asked. "I have some books if you'd like to borrow one."

"What would you like to do?" Alta glanced from him to Fannie.

Jonas rubbed the back of his neck. "Whatever you want."

"It's been a long day. Can we sit in the other room for a time?" Alta stood and began to gather plates and utensils.

Fannie got up immediately. "Alta, you don't have to do that."

"Please. You have both been *wunderbor*. Let me pull my weight. I don't mind doing the dishes." Alta brought a stack to the sink then grabbed the bottle of dish detergent and squirted some into the basin before turning on the water.

"Alta, it's not necessary," his daughter began.

"To me, it is." Alta flashed her a smile as she returned to the table to gather what needed to be washed and put away.

"I'll dry," Jonas said as he rose from his chair and went to the sink.

"Jonas, you don't have to do women's work," Alta protested.

He opened a drawer and grabbed a dish towel. "I do it all the time, Alta."

"*Dat*—"

"Why don't you pull out some books for Alta to look at?" Jonas responded. "You cooked."

"I know, but—" One look at his expression was warning enough for Fannie to obey.

Alta washed a dish and he dried it. She did several plates and utensils, and Jonas grabbed one and wiped it with the towel.

Fannie grabbed the towel out of her father's hands. "*Dat*, you're exhausted. Please. Go into the other room and relax. I'll take over drying. You can pick out some books for Alta to choose from."

Feeling tired suddenly, Jonas agreed. He entered the great room, stoked up the fire in the woodstove then pulled several books from the shelf. Unsure of what Alta might like to read, he chose a book on gardening, a few other nonfiction books, and two fiction books that his children enjoyed after they were old enough to finish school. He set them on the small table between two chairs. Then he sat down on the sofa to wait for Fannie and Alta to join him and closed his eyes for a minute.

Seeing how tired Jonas appeared, Alta was glad he gave in and went into the other room.

He didn't need to be doing dishes, especially not with two women willing to do the work.

She and Fannie chatted as they finished cleaning the kitchen.

"How many *bruders* do you have?" she asked the young woman.

Fannie smiled as she hung up the damp dish towel. "Three *bruders* and one *schweschter*." She put away the rest of the pie. "Davy and Danny are twins," she said. "They are single, run a business and share a house. My eldest *bruder* Joshua and his family live in Manheim Township. They are struggling with whether to stay there since contractors have been building homes for the English and other businesses have been popping up all over their community. Joshua worries about the effect of traffic on safe travel. I got a letter from him recently. He said he's considering moving back here to New Berne." She held up an iced tea pitcher. "Refill?" Alta nodded. "Well, to continue with my siblings, my sister Sadie is married and lives in lower Lebanon County close to the Lancaster County northern border in an area called Mount Gretna."

Alta was familiar with Mount Gretna, a rural Amish community with narrow dirt roads and a quiet life. "It must have been great to grow up with that many siblings," she said. "My parents only had Lovina and me. They wanted more children, but my *mudder* couldn't have any more." She recalled how disappointed her father had been that he'd never had a son.

Alta wiped the table while Fannie took care of the countertops and then she went with the younger woman into the great room. The first thing she saw was Jonas sitting on the wooden-frame sofa, his head back, eyes closed, sound asleep. Studying him lying sleeping so peacefully, something stirred deep inside of her. Alta wished she could have more with him. What would be like to have Jonas as her husband? Glancing away, she exchanged understanding looks with his daughter.

"He's been up since before dawn," Fannie whispered.

Alta nodded. "And he was busy at the fund-raiser," she murmured.

"We'll let him rest. I'll wake him later and urge him to head up to bed." Fannie waved her to follow. "Come with me and I'll show you where you'll be spending the night."

After glancing back once at Jonas's sleeping form, Alta trailed Fannie toward the stairs to the second floor, her thoughts lingering on the handsome widower who had captured her attention and tugged on her heartstrings.

There were three upstairs bedrooms and a

bathroom. Fannie gave her a tour of the upstairs before she brought her to the room with
two single beds. "This is where you'll be sleeping. That's my bed," she said. "I used to share
with my *schweschter.* The other room besides
my *dat's* belonged to my *bruders,* who took
their beds with them when they moved into
their house."

Alta studied the room and smiled. There
were colorful quilts on both beds. *"Danki."*
She wondered what she would wear to sleep in.

"You're *willkomm.*" She went to a dresser
and pulled a garment out of a drawer. "This
may be a little big on you but it should work for
tonight," Fannie said, handing her a nightgown.

Nodding, Alta was overcome with emotion
over the generosity of Fannie and her father.
"I… I appreciate this."

Fannie smiled. "I'll get us some extra blan-
kets. It's gotten colder than we expected. *Dat*
fed the fire in the woodstove and that will help,
but it's best we're prepared in case we get chilly
during the night." After she left the room, she
returned minutes later with soft gray cover-
ings. "Feel free to use the bathroom first. I put
out fresh linens for you. I'll head downstairs to
check on *Dat.*" Fannie was gone only a few seconds when she dipped her head inside. "Would

you like a mug of hot chocolate before you go to bed? It always helps me sleep."

Hot chocolate sounded nice. Alta needed to sleep, and while she was tired, she would also be sleeping in a room in a house that wasn't her own or her sister's. Any help to lull her to sleep would be appreciated. "*Danki.* I'd love some."

Nodding, Fannie departed. Alta heard the woman's treads on the steps as Fannie headed downstairs. Eager to avoid any embarrassing situations, Alta went into the bathroom, quickly washed and dressed before she went back to Fannie's room where she climbed into bed, slipped under the covers and saw that Fannie had left a battery lamp lit for her.

Fannie entered with two mugs of hot chocolate and handed one to Alta. "I hope you like whipped cream," she said.

Alta nodded. "Love it." She took a small sip since she knew it was hot. "Delicious. *Danki,* Fannie."

"My pleasure." She set another mug on the nightstand near her bed. "I'll be back shortly. I'm going to wake *Dat* and get him to come upstairs."

Trying not to think of the man sleeping peacefully on the couch downstairs, Alta plumped up her pillow behind her then continued to enjoy her hot chocolate. Moments later, she heard Fannie and Jonas's conversation as they ascended the stairs together.

"I could have stayed downstairs," Jonas said, sounding weary.

"And then wake up with a sore back. *Nay, Dat*. I can't have you doing that. I put a mug of hot chocolate for you in your room. It won't take you long to get back to sleep."

"You're a *gut dochter*, Fannie," Jonas said, and Alta heard the affection in his voice.

"Gut nacht, Dat."

"Gut nacht, Fannie."

Jonas's deep voice made Alta think about all the years she'd lived without a man in the house—with John in the house. It made her feel lonely and long for something she'd never have. A man like Jonas Miller, a preacher in the Amish church. She blinked back tears as she gazed up at the ceiling. For years, she desperately missed her late husband, although her daughters had filled a large part of her heart. But now she didn't have them to comfort her. Unwilling to be a burden to her sister and her family, Alta had no idea what to do next.

After finishing her hot chocolate, she set the mug on her nightstand then readjusted her pillow and lay down. Fannie came in moments later, dressed in a nightgown she must have placed in another room where the young woman could access it easily.

She felt comfortable in Jonas's house and with his daughter. *Please, Lord, give me Your guidance. Help me to know what to do.* Should she stay or move on? Lovina seemed happy for now to have her stay. And then there was Jonas, a man she enjoyed spending time with.

Chapter Nine

The sun shone through the window when Alta stirred in bed and sat up. Looking toward Fannie's side of the room, she realized by the neatly made bed that Jonas's daughter was up and about. *I'm a terrible guest!* She should be downstairs helping with breakfast. Grabbing her watch from the nightstand, she saw that it was nine o'clock, and she was embarrassed for sleeping in. Pushing aside the sheer curtains, Alta looked out into the yard. Her breath caught at nature's beauty with snow glistening on the trees and side yard.

What about the roads?

Alta hurriedly dressed, fixed her hair then donned her head covering. What must Jonas think of her? And Fannie? She should have woken up earlier to help make breakfast. Tears filled her eyes. She felt out of sorts with so much happening ever since she'd arrived nearly three weeks ago. Alta headed down the staircase and entered the kitchen. Fannie was at the stove cooking eggs and bacon.

When she caught sight of her, Jonas's daughter glanced at her with a smile. "*Gut* morning, Alta."

"*Gut mariga,* Fannie. I overslept and I apologize for not coming down sooner." A glance toward the table showed three place settings. Alta frowned. "Haven't you eaten?"

"*Nay.* We haven't been up long ourselves."

Alta held onto hope. "You haven't?"

Fannie shook her head. "Woke up a half hour ago. I guess we were all more tired than we thought." She grabbed the coffeepot from the stove. "Coffee?"

"*Ja. Danki.*" Alta accepted a filled mug from Fannie. "What can I do to help?"

"Not a thing. Everything is about ready. Have a seat," Fannie said as she moved a pan from a burner to a hot mat on the counter. "Just waiting for *Dat.*"

"Where is your *vadder*?" Alta asked, her heart beating wildly as she thought of Jonas. She sat down at the kitchen table, choosing the same spot she'd been in for a meal late yesterday.

"Lovina might have told you that ours is a

dairy farm. *Dat*'s milking then feeding our cows since we can't turn them out to pasture with the snow." Fannie used tongs to take the bacon from the frying pan onto a paper towel-lined plate. "He should be in soon for breakfast."

Glancing back at the table then to the stove, Alta felt the need to help. "Isn't there anything I can do?" She saw a loaf of homemade bread on the counter as if waiting to be served. "Would you like me to slice the bread?"

"*Ja,* that would be *gut.* Would you please get the strawberry and blackberry jams out of the refrigerator? The butter is already on the table." Fannie scrambled eggs in the pan of bacon grease then scooped them out when they were ready.

Before she sliced the bread, Alta brought the two types of jam to the table. The kitchen smelled inviting. Jonas must have stoked the fire in this room and the great room, for the house was warm and cozy. "How are the roads this morning?" she asked as she cut then placed the slices into a cloth-lined wicker basket.

"The streets were plowed and salted during the night," Fannie said as she stirred the batter for flapjacks. "Usually, the trucks are loud enough to wake me, but I must have slept hard because I didn't hear a thing."

"Me neither," Alta said as she worked with the bread. "Do you want the whole loaf sliced or is this enough?"

Fannie looked over. "That's fine."

The stomp of feet on the stoop drew Alta's attention.

"There's Dat now."

The door opened and Jonas appeared. "I smell pancakes!"

"They will be ready in a minute." Fannie smiled as she flipped a flapjack.

He grinned when he saw her. "*Gut morning, Alta!* Did you sleep well?"

Alta nodded. "So, well I overslept. That's not like me."

His gaze warmed. "We all did. It was a busy day yesterday."

"*Ja,* it was, but I've never slept that well after a busy day before." Alta realized what she said and turned away as a tingle ran the length of her spine

"Unusual circumstances then," Jonas said as he moved closer, startling her when he washed his hands at the kitchen sink.

"I hear the roads were plowed." Alta moved to place the basket of bread on the table.

"*Ja.* I should be able to take you home." He gazed at her as he used a hand towel to dry his hands. "There is some snow left, but the rest will melt with the sun."

Alta nodded. She realized that she soon would be back with Lovina, and the thought didn't bring much comfort, because she liked him more than she should. Now that they were no longer working on the fundraiser together, she would only see him on church Sundays and perhaps on an occasional Visiting Day.

Fannie turned from the stove with a dish of pancakes and a bottle of syrup. "Breakfast!" she announced with a smile before she set the platter within everyone's reach. She went back for the bacon and eggs.

Jonas took a chair then forked up two pancakes and offered them to Alta.

"Danki," she said as she held up her plate. Her eyes widened as she spied chocolate chips mixed in. "Fannie, I love chocolate chip pancakes."

Jonas's daughter chuckled. *"Dat* said it was your idea to offer them as a choice at the fundraiser."

"Ja, because I like them so much," Alta replied with a grin. Pleasantly surprised, she spread butter over each sides of the flapjacks. "They smell and look delicious." Chocolate chip pancakes brought back happy memories

of when she and John were married. He'd loved the ones she'd made for him.

After handing her the pitcher of syrup, Jonas took two flapjacks for himself. He used butter and syrup on them and then grabbed some scrambled eggs and bacon.

Alta ate quietly while listening to Jonas and Fannie talk about the farm and the weather. She had no idea if they were in for another snowfall, but it wouldn't matter because Alta knew she'd be back at Lovina's house before it arrived.

When each of them was done eating, Alta got up and began clearing the table.

"Sit, Alta." Fannie smiled and gestured for her to remain seated. "There's no rush for that."

"*Ja,* Alta, relax and enjoy another cup of coffee with us," Jonas said as he went to pick up the pot from the stove. "We'll leave in about an hour. By then the streets will be clear enough to drive safely on."

At his urging, Alta sat. It wasn't as if she had any clothes to pack. Then she thought that she could help with the laundry. "Would you like me to put the wash on?" she asked, starting to rise.

"*Nay.*" Jonas set her coffee on the table before her. "Alta, please. We want to enjoy your company before I take you home."

Did he enjoy her company? Hearing him

suggest that he did was startling and appreciated. Alta beamed at him. She liked him a lot but couldn't allow herself to think of anything more.

Alta added a word here and there as Jonas and Fannie continued to discuss his dairy farm and Fannie's Luncheonette. How much richer their lives were than hers. *I need a purpose.* Wherever she went, whether home or somewhere else, she needed to find something worthwhile to give back to the community. After her husband had died, she had lived for her girls, and after they'd married, she still hadn't done anything else but gossip. She regretted her behavior these last eleven years. Alta had never meant to hurt anyone, but ultimately, she had.

The rumble of a motor and the scraping sound of metal drew her and the other's attention. Jonas went outside to check and came back only a short time later.

"The snowplow just went through again," he announced. "I can take you home safely now."

"Danki," she murmured as she rose then began to clear the table. "I appreciate your hospitality. You've been kind to me, and I won't forget it."

Jonas came up to the table to help her. "You are easy to be kind to, Alta."

* * *

The ride toward Lovina's house was silent. Concerned, Jonas glanced frequently toward her. He had enjoyed having her in his house, seeing her smile and eating meals with him. What was she thinking? If only he knew.

The Adam King property loomed up ahead on the right. Jonas made the turn onto the lane carefully, as the driveway was still covered with snow. Today was Visiting Sunday, but he doubted that anyone except for him would venture from home.

"Alta," he said softly as he parked his buggy close to the residence, "*danki* for your help yesterday. I couldn't have done the fundraiser without you."

She faced him, looking doubtful. "I'm sure there are other women within your community who are more than capable of handling the job."

"I think not," he replied. "You stepped right up in planning the event, and everyone looked to you for guidance yesterday." He paused and turned in his seat toward her. "Alta, I enjoyed working with you, having you in my home. You are truly an amazing woman."

Jonas saw her eyes dim before Alta looked down at her lap. She shook her head then met his gaze. "I'm not the person you think I am."

"I don't believe that." There was something about this woman that continued to pull him in. The thought of not seeing her again alarmed him. But for now, she was staying in New Berne, and he would make sure he was a frequent visitor. Given how frightened she was riding in the snow yesterday, he didn't think she'd be going anywhere anytime soon.

As if to reinforce his thoughts, he saw snow flurries in the air. "Please stay in your seat," he said. Jonas got out of the buggy and carefully rounded the vehicle, slipping a little once before he reached the passenger side. He opened the door and reached in to help. "It's a bit slippery."

Alta stared at his extended hand. Finally, she placed her fingers within his grasp and allowed him to assist her from the buggy. He walked with her to the house and knocked on the door. After a few seconds, Lovina appeared with a relieved look and a wide smile on her face.

"Alta, I'm glad to have you home. Jonas, *danki* for taking such *gut* care of her." She stepped back to allow them entry. "Preacher, stay for coffee?"

He remained on the stoop and shook his head. "*Nay,* I appreciate the invitation, but I should get back. It's starting to flurry, and I have a feeling that it's going to snow hard again."

Adam appeared behind his wife. "Jonas, how are the roads?"

"Not bad, but only because they've been plowed and salted." Jonas watched as Alta slipped inside. Lovina left, allowing Adam and him to talk. "I know it's Visiting Sunday, but the way the sky looks, I think we can expect another few inches."

Adam nodded and opened the door. "Are you sure you won't stay for a bit?"

"*Ja,* I'm sure. Fannie is home by herself. While the roads aren't bad, the shoulders along the side aren't the best, and whenever a car passes, it can be worrisome." Jonas tried to look past Adam to see Alta. "But I'll be happy to take a rain check," he said and laughed. "Or should I say snow check?" His gaze met Adam's, and he caught the flicker of amusement in the man's bright blue eyes.

"Consider this an open invitation," Adam said. "*Danki* for taking care of Lovina's *schweschter.*"

"It was my pleasure," Jonas admitted candidly. He lowered his voice so that only Adam could hear. "She is an amazing woman who doesn't know her worth. I hope to do something about that."

Adam nodded. "As a minister or someone else?"

"My position as a preacher has nothing to do with my intentions."

Alta's brother-in-law grinned. "*Gut.* I'd hoped you'd say that."

A few minutes later, Jonas was trying to turn around in the driveway but got stuck. Adam and two of his sons appeared with shovels and dug his wheels from a snowdrift and cleared an area for him to complete the maneuver with a little extra to get him going.

Adam came to his side of the buggy as his sons went to put the shovels in the barn. "Sorry about that. A friend is supposed to plow this for us, but he's a little late. I'm sure ours is not the only one that needs digging out."

"It's fine," Jonas said warmly. "I appreciate the help. Take care of your family."

The other man nodded. "I'll take care of them," he said with a teasing glimmer, "and her."

Once he was on the main road, Jonas found the drive back easy. He was eager to get home, yet he'd been tempted to stay after Lovina had invited him in. The church elders had been pressing him again to marry, and he'd been vehement that he wouldn't wed without love. But ever since he'd met and come to know Alta Hershberger, he'd found himself open to the idea of marrying again.

It's been long enough. Everyone has been telling me so. Jonas knew it would take time to earn Alta's trust. Thankfully, he was a patient man, and while she was in New Berne, he'd find a way to win her over. His community was right. It was time for him to move forward and to love again.

Jonas hoped and prayed that Alta wouldn't decide to leave before he had the chance to convince her to stay in his life permanently.

Chapter Ten

Visiting Day was quiet in her sister's household. The snow continued to fall, blanketing land and roads, keeping everyone inside. Alta gazed at her nieces and nephews, marveling how thoughtful they were as everyone sat together in the great room. Since it was a Sunday, the family was playing Dutch Blitz, reading, doing a puzzle or simply resting with their eyes closed.

Alta liked spending time in New Berne with Lovina. Her sister had a life much different than her own. She wasn't jealous; she was grateful that her only sibling had found happiness with Adam.

She sighed, worried, as it hit her that there would come a time soon when she would have to think about going home. Alta didn't want to overstay her welcome, but if Lovina asked her to remain through the winter, she would accept happily. She liked it in this Amish community. Her sister and family were here, and then there was Jonas. If she confessed why she was reluctant to head back to Happiness, would he understand? Or would the preacher judge and find her lacking?

It had only been a few hours since Jonas had left. Alta missed him and longed to see him again. After John's death, Alta never thought she'd find another man she felt she could trust, a man she was drawn to. The realization that she cared deeply about Jonas shook her. Spending the night, interacting with Jonas and his daughter in their home, had been more than enjoyable.

When the church had urged her to marry only months after her husband's death, Alta had been reluctant. Pressure from her community made her think about having another man in her life. And that was when Abner Renno had come calling. He'd been charming. When he'd pushed hard to make her his bride, Alta had begun to have a bad feeling about him. She'd refused to let him press her into something she wasn't sure she wanted to do. And then she'd found out that he'd known about the cash settlement she was awarded after John's death. Alta didn't confront him at first. She watched him in her home and around her daughters, and she hadn't liked the way he'd been eyeing her beautiful teenage girls. The decision not to marry had come to her easily after that. When he'd asked her to marry him again, she'd said *nay*. And she'd suffered the consequences of the man's anger and realized that she'd narrowly escaped a horrible life with the vengeful man. Alta had gone to see the bishop the next day, and not long afterward Abner had left Happiness for good.

Alta shivered and hugged herself. The memory still had the power to scare her. She didn't know why it was bothering her again now. Was it because of her friendship with Jonas?

"*Endie* Alta, would you like to play Dutch Blitz with us?" Isaiah said.

Shaking herself from her dark thoughts, Alta managed a smile. "*Nay*, but I'd love to watch while you play."

Watching her nieces and nephews play Dutch Blitz, a popular card game in the Amish community, made Alta relax and smile. Linda and Esther teased their brothers. The boys—young men—joked with their sisters in return, much to Alta's amusement.

Later that day she and Lovina provided a simple supper, and the family dined on roast beef and ham sandwiches. Soon darkness descended, and Adam switched on a battery lantern. Not long afterward the family headed upstairs for bed.

Not the least bit sleepy, Alta sat for a few minutes after everyone left for their rooms. She turned toward the window and watched the snowfall. Grabbing the flashlight Lovina had given her, she made her way to the kitchen. Wide awake, she knew she would have trouble getting to sleep. Thoughts of her past—most recent and during the early years of being a widow—came back to haunt her. She closed her eyes and thought of Jonas Miller…and sighed with relief. Thinking of Jonas was much more welcomed than memories of Abner.

A hot, sweetened cup of milk would help her sleep. It was her favorite drink when she needed to relax. She pulled a mug from a kitchen cupboard and milk from the refrigerator. The sugar bowl was already on the counter.

While the milk heated, Alta thought back to her childhood when she and Lovina used to drink milk together late at night. As if her mind had called out to her, Lovina entered the kitchen with the battery-operated lantern. "Hot sweetened milk," Lovina murmured with a smile. "Care to sit and enjoy it like we used to?"

Alta nodded. "I put in a little extra in case you joined me." She took the pan off the heat and poured the milk into two mugs and fixed it the way she and Lovina had liked it when they were young.

Her sister pulled out a kitchen chair and sat down. "I often enjoy hot milk," Lovina said with a sad smile. "Only it's never been the same without you."

"I'm sorry." Alta took the seat next to her.

"You have nothing to apologize for." Lovina cradled the warm mug. "The fault was mine, not yours," she insisted. "I was jealous. It was clear that Johnathan loved you. I had a terrible crush on him, and I allowed it to ruin our relationship." She hung her head and stared at the milk. "I'm sorry, Alta. I reacted badly, and I've missed you since I left."

Reaching over the table, Alta covered Lovina's hand with her own. "I'm happy we've had this time together."

"I am, too," her sister said with a warm smile.

Alta bit her lip as she worried about staying. Unwilling to be a burden to Lovina and her family, she took a sip from her mug and then set it down, bracing herself for what she had to say. "Lovina, the weather has taken a turn for the worse. I didn't expect winter weather to arrive so early. I don't want to impose so maybe I should go."

"*Nay.*" Lovina looked alarmed. "Please! Stay

the winter. Do you need to call someone to check on your *haus*?"

"I turned off the water before I left," Alta admitted. "I could always call Miriam and ask her to check on it for me."

Lovina grinned. "That would be *wunderbor!* I want to spend more time with you. My family loves you." She paused and eyed her affectionately. "I missed you more than you'll ever know."

Her heart melting at her sister's confession, Alta studied Lovina's expression, convinced that her sister wanted her to stay. "If you get tired of me, please let me know. I don't want to be a burden." She could hire someone to drive her home. While she had driven her buggy to New Berne, she refused to drive in winter weather.

"I'll not get tired of you, *schweschter.*" Concern entered Lovina's expression. "You would never be a burden, but you work too hard. Do you realize how much work you've done since you've arrived?" She took a sip of hot milk. "But what about Mary and Sally? Won't they be upset if you don't go back?"

Alta shook her head. "*Nay.* They have busy lives. I doubt they're missing me." She ignored her sibling's questioning look. "Besides, I'll see them when the weather warms in the spring."

Head tilted, Lovina reached across the table, placing her hand over Alta's. "*Schweschter*... about your girls. Are they reason you decided to visit now? Did something happen between you?"

"I'm sorry, Lovina. I can't talk about it right now," Alta replied with tears in her eyes. "But please know that I came because I wanted to see you again."

Lovina gave her hand a brief squeeze. "I'm glad you're staying."

"I am, too," Alta whispered. "*Danki* for having me here." She drank a taste of hot milk.

"I should have written," her sister said, her eyes filling with tears. "I'm so sorry. There are no *gut* excuses for why I didn't. Life was busy, but our relationship is important."

Alta set the mug on the table. "We're fine now." There were only the two of them. Their mother had been unable to have another child. It had hurt when things went badly between her and Lovina. She was grateful she had her sister back and that Lovina felt the same way. "I don't know about you, but I think this is helping," she said before she emptied her cup. "I believe I'm tired enough to sleep."

Lovina nodded. "Me, too." She drank the last drop then stood with her mug and reached for

Alta's. "Jonas thinks a lot of you," she said as she brought them to the sink to wash.

"I doubt that, but *danki* for believing it." Alta stood and grabbed a towel to dry them. "I doubt we'll see much of him now that the fundraiser is over."

"He's close to our family," Lovina said as she emptied the washbasin. "You haven't seen the last of him."

Her mind filling with images of Jonas, Alta hung up the dish towel. *"Gut nacht, schweschter."*

She followed her sister upstairs, and once in bed, she couldn't stop thinking about Jonas. He was a man unlike any other. As much as she'd loved John, Alta found herself appreciating the minister for himself. Jonas was willing to work in the kitchen, to help a friend and member of his Amish community…and he'd been more than kind to her. Releasing a sharp breath, Alta knew she had to stop hoping for more with him. There were things he didn't know about her past, and she was afraid that once he did, he would think less of her. And the last thing she wanted was to see him regarding her with a frown instead of a smile.

"I have to go, *Dat*," Fannie said. "I know the streets are snowy, but the English are still out and about in their cars and will come to my luncheonette to eat."

"I don't know, *dochter*," Jonas replied with concern. He sat across from Fannie in the kitchen as they finished their morning cups of coffee. "I hate to see you travel on these roads. It snowed a great deal overnight."

Fannie stood and collected the breakfast dishes. "I know, but I heard the snowplows. I'll be *oll recht* to drive over there."

"I'd feel better if you let me take you." At his daughter's narrowed look, Jonas shook his head. "I'm not saying that you're not capable. I…you're my *dochter.* I already lost your *mam.* Please let me bring you this morning and pick you up after the restaurant closes."

Fannie started to wash and rinse a dish before placing it on the drain rack. "You don't need to be out and about."

Jonas put away the milk and the jam he'd had on his bread this morning. "I thought I'd stop by Adam King's," he murmured.

"*Ach*, you want to see Alta again." Fannie's lips twitched. "That's why. So, *ja,* you can drive me to work if you'd like."

"Fannie—" he protested as he dried a dish and put it away.

"She is a nice woman. Lovely and kind-hearted," his daughter said. "I think she'll be *gut* for you."

He felt guilty as if he'd somehow betrayed Lena. "But your *mam*—"

Fannie stopped what she was doing and faced him. "*Dat*, we all miss her, but you need to move on with your life. You deserve happiness. It's been five long years!" Her expression softened as she placed a hand on his arm. "*Mam* would have wanted this for you."

Although he'd wanted Alta permanently in his life, he couldn't help but worry how his children, even as grown as they were, would handle him seeing another woman. Jonas sighed heavily. Fannie seemed to like the idea. Would the others like it, too?

"*Dat*, I won't always be living here with you," Fannie said as she withdrew her hand to wipe down the counter. "You know that. Alta... I think she is lonely, and I've seen how she looks at you. She likes you. A lot."

"*Ja?*" Jonas felt a frisson of hope.

"*Ja.*" She placed her dishrag over the rack near the sink then took the towel from him and hung it up. "I must leave in a few minutes. Will you be able to take me then?"

He nodded. "I'll get the buggy ready." He saw his daughter nod before she turned to leave the room. "Fannie."

She halted and glanced back. *"Ja?"*

"Danki, dochter." He eyed her with affection. She was a lot like her mother in looks, but their personalities were different. Fannie was strong and determined enough to open her restaurant, no easy feat, while Lena had been soft…less inclined to believe in herself to venture out to try new things and find a place of her own within the community. Lena had been content to be his wife and a mother to his children. She'd never attended a quilting bee or sewing circle yet had seemed happy in her life with him.

Jonas readied the carriage and waited patiently for his daughter to join him outside. Fannie came out of the house and locked up. When she turned, she was grinning. "Thought it best if we don't leave the *haus* open since we'll both be gone for some time." She sprang up and into the carriage while he got in more slowly.

"You have everything you need?" Jonas asked, tugging his navy woolen cap down over his ears.

"Ja." She had dressed warmly in her black winter coat and black bonnet over her prayer *kapp*. She wore the same color scarf around her neck and across her chin.

There was a brisk breeze tossing the evening's snow across the roof and yard. Whenever a stronger gust blew up, it hampered the visibility of the road. But to Jonas's surprise, the road wasn't as bad as he'd thought. He was careful to stay on the side of the street where the plows had cleared away the snow onto the embankment on the edge of farmers' fields.

Ten minutes later, Jonas guided his horse into the parking lot next to Fannie's building. He stopped the vehicle and got out to tie up his mare. Fannie climbed out the other side.

"*Dat*, I'll bring home supper," Fannie told him. "So don't worry about cooking for yourself. If I'm running a little late, grab a snack from the refrigerator. I cut up some cheese and there is some bread left from yesterday. Either one or both should hold you over."

"I shouldn't need a snack," Jonas said. "What time do you want me to pick you up?"

"Five?" Fannie unlocked the back door of her restaurant. "I don't know if I'll be done by then, but you won't have too long to wait. If you'd prefer, you could eat here."

Jonas followed his daughter inside. He wanted to make sure everything was all right after the snowstorm blew in. Fannie flipped on the light. It was a little chilly inside the main dining room but it wouldn't be for long. The restaurant had gas heat. She turned the thermostat up to a comfortable level then headed to the kitchen to turn on the oven.

"Everything looks *gut* in here, *Dat*," she told him. "No need for you to worry or stay."

He took a moment to look at the space that Fannie had made into a cozy, wonderful place to eat. "I'll head to the Kings' then," he told her. "Call Esther if you have a problem or need anything."

"I will." Fannie faced her father with a wide smile. "Enjoy your day with Alta."

Shaking his head, Jonas frowned at his daughter. "I don't know that this will go anywhere."

"If you never try, it most definitely won't. So go and spend time with her, *Vadder*. You deserve a second chance at love."

Jonas blinked. "Love?"

Fannie eyed him with amusement. "Eventually," she said. "Now go. You're wasting daylight."

He laughed. "Have a *gut* day, Fannie. Remember to call if you need anything."

With his daughter's "I will" ringing in his ear as he left, Jonas turned his attention to his visit to Adam King's family...and Alta Hershberger, the woman who had taken up a lot of space in his mind and stolen a piece of his heart.

Adam's driveway had been plowed recently

so it was easy enough for Jonas's buggy to enter the property and park. After he tied up his horse, he approached the house. The curtains were closed, and as he looked up, he saw that the shades were drawn.

Jonas hesitated. He didn't want to wake them. As he climbed up the stoop's two steps, he thought about the one woman inside that he wanted to see. Two light taps on the door in case the household was still asleep. He waited and was about to leave when the door swung open.

"Jonas!" Alta greeted. "How did you get here? Aren't the roads icy?"

"They've been plowed and salted so they aren't as bad as they were." He smiled at her. "*Gut mariga*, Alta." Jonas kept his voice quiet. "Is everyone up and about? I can leave if they're sleeping. I took Fannie to the restaurant and decided to stop by."

"Everyone is awake except Lovina's *kinner who* are still in their bedrooms. Adam, Lovina and I came downstairs a couple of hours ago." Alta stepped back so Jonas could enter. "Adam went out to the barn. Lovina is checking on her Rhode Island Red hens. Please come in. I put a fresh pot of coffee on. Would you like a cup?"

"*Ja, danki.*" A frequent visitor to the house, Jonas pulled out a chair and sat down. "After coffee, would you like to take a ride with me?"

Alta turned with a coffee cup in hand. "You want me to go for a ride?" She looked stunned by the invitation.

"Ja." Jonas accepted the coffee with a smile. "You'll be safe with me." He took a sip from his cup. "This coffee is just the way I like it."

Adam entered the house and grinned when he saw Jonas seated at the table. *"Hallo,* Jonas. Glad to see you. I take it the roads are much better than they were."

"Gut mariga, Adam. *Ja,* I took Fannie to the restaurant because I didn't want her driving on her own."

Lovina came in moments later from checking on the chickens. "What a lovely surprise!"

As he interacted with his friends, Jonas observed Alta pouring two more cups of coffee. She handed one to Adam and another to her sister. Each nodded their thanks and continued to talk about the snowstorm and the conditions.

"The fundraiser made over $5,000," Jonas told them during a lull when they had exhausted the topic of the weather.

"How *wunderbor*!" Lovina exclaimed. They discussed the success of the event until suddenly Lovina shot her sister a look, which made Alta look away and shift in her seat, clearly uncomfortable. "Is anything wrong?"

Alta shook her head. *"Nay."*

"I've asked Alta if she'd like to take a ride with me," Jonas said, his gaze centered on Alta.

Lovina grinned. "I'm sure she'd enjoy it."

Jonas could barely keep his eyes off Alta. "She hasn't given me an answer yet." She blushed, and her red cheeks made her more beautiful.

"*Schweschter,* don't you want to go?" Lovina asked softly.

"I…the roads…" Alta appeared flustered.

"You have nothing to worry about," Jonas told her.

There was a large rumble of an engine and the scraping sound of steel against blacktop heralded the arrival of a snowplow as it went past again. Lovina left the room and returned less than a minute later. "Roads are clear," she announced with a smile for Alta and then for him.

"Alta?" Jonas softened his expression as he saw Alta struggle with how to answer. "Say *ja.*"

She locked gazes with him. The air seemed charged until Alta glanced away briefly. *"Ja,"* she said quietly as she looked at him.

Jonas grinned. "We can eat at Fannie's for lunch."

Alta blinked, wariness in her green eyes. "Lovina, do you need me to do anything? Wash? Clean house?"

"*Nay*," Lovina said. "I think we're caught up right now. Esther can do any housework that may need to be done. She cleans houses to earn money now."

"*Gut!*" Jonas announced, feeling like a young boy who had been offered ice cream on a hot summer's day. Sensing that she was nervous, he sat back to leisurely drink his coffee, his gaze on pretty, silent Alta Hershberger, the woman he would like to spend time with and get to know.

Chapter Eleven

Snow glistened along the roadside. The plowed paved streets were clear, the sun already warm enough to melt the rest of the ice and snow mixture. Alta sat on the bench seat next to Jonas, thoughts whirling through her head. *Why did he come to visit? Does he need my help with something? Or is it because he wants to see me? What will I do if he likes me as more than a friend?*

She worried about how Jonas saw her. Alta liked him more than a lot, but she doubted there could ever be a long-term relationship between them. Because if he learned the truth, she was afraid that he'd want nothing to do with her. And she couldn't bear to endure his rejection. If her daughters believed the worst of her, why should Jonas be any different?

"I thought we'd make a stop at Kings General Store first," Jonas said, interrupting her chaotic musings. "Fannie needs a few groceries for her eatery." His quick grin toward her made her catch her breath. "I was hoping you wouldn't mind assisting me."

Relieved, Alta smiled. She was here because he needed her help, not because he was interested in her. Her relief turned to disappointment that Jonas didn't simply want to spend time with her. "Not at all. I'll be happy to shop with you. Do you have a list?"

"*Ja,* Fannie was most specific. She usually does the shopping herself, but with the fundraiser and then the snow..."

Jonas came to the end of the road that her sister lived on, then made a left toward Kings General Store. In the three weeks that she'd been in New Berne, Alta had yet to shop there. She was eager to see inside. Was it as good as the one in Happiness? Not that she could afford much shopping with the money she'd brought with her.

It didn't take long to get there, and Alta was glad that the lot beside the store had been plowed, the sun quickly melting what was left of the snow. There were already other buggies parked there.

"If you wait a moment, I'll come around to help you get out," Jonas said, ever the thoughtful, kind man. Something shifted in her chest.

She knew she liked him, but there were times like now when she wished she was free to have more than friendship. Wanting was one thing, she thought, but having was another.

Soon, Alta and Jonas entered the building. There was a counter with a cash register up front, to the right of the door. Straight ahead were shelves of every kind of food and other household merchandise, the like of what she'd never seen before. Kings had a section for medicinal items such as menthol cream used for sore muscles and joints, although her people often made use of vinegar water first. There were boxes of Goody's headache powder and small bottles of ibuprofen.

"Morning, Jed," Jonas greeted the man behind the register. "Snow affecting business?"

Jed smiled. "*Gut* to see you, Jonas. At first, the store was slow, but it's picked up some with the roads clear again." His gaze went to Alta. "Who do we have here?" He blinked. "Wait, you're Alta Hershberger, Lovina's sister, *ja*?"

Alta nodded. "I am. Sorry I haven't been in sooner."

"You're here now," Jed pointed out.

"Fannie gave Jonas a shopping list," she explained pleasantly. "I'm here to help him shop for her." She sensed Jonas's frown before she met his gaze.

"Alta…"

"May I have the list?" she asked, wondering what he was going to say but afraid at the same time to find out he didn't want to shop as much as he wanted her company. She liked Jonas a lot but it was better that they remained friends and nothing more.

Jonas took a folded piece of paper from under his woolen hat then handed it to her. He waited patiently for her to look over it.

There were five things on the list. Nothing that would take up much of anyone's time to find, and Alta knew for a fact that Jonas had shopped alone for groceries the day she'd met him. Puzzled, she eyed him with raised eyebrows before she started to look for the five simple items that Fannie needed.

Jonas fell into step with her. Fannie needed flour, so Alta saw the sign and went down the baking aisle. "What kind should we get?" he asked. "Is one brand any better than the other?"

Alta shook her head. "The list has flour on it, but not how much. Did she tell you what she wanted?"

"*Nay.* Maybe if we buy her three five-pound bags?"

She grinned. "That sounds like a fine idea. She can open them up as she needs them. You can always buy more for her later."

He looked relieved. "Now what?" he asked since she held the list.

"Sugar."

After placing the same amount of sugar as flour in a cart, Jonas and she found the other things on the list. Soon, they stood near the register as Jed rang up their purchase.

The bells on the front entrance door jingled. Alta turned and froze, recognizing the man who entered the store. She started to tremble, wanting to escape before he saw her.

"Are you ready to go?" Jonas asked.

She nodded and hurried out of the store, waiting near the buggy as Jonas carried the groceries out to the vehicle and set them on the back seat. Alta hugged herself and began to shake uncontrollably.

He faced her. "What's wrong?" Jonas asked with concern.

"I'm fine." She managed to smile at him although she wanted nothing more than to leave and get home.

"You're not fine. You're shaking like a leaf." He stepped closer and placed his hand on her shoulder.

Alta jerked, her gaze flying to the door, afraid that Abner would see her before she had a chance to get away. "Can we leave?"

Jonas frowned. "*Ja*. Alta—"

"I'm *okey*, Jonas." She moved to get in. Jonas captured her by the waist and lifted her, setting her carefully on the bench seat, startling her. He remained standing by her door as she got comfortable. When she looked up, she saw his concern for her. "Are you *oll recht*?" she asked softly.

He didn't answer. His eyes continued to hold hers. "That should be my question for you." He didn't move away. "What happened? You look like you saw something or someone who upset you."

"Jonas—" She sighed. "I'm just ready to leave."

Without demanding an answer to his question, he climbed into the driver's side. Her relief was so great that she managed a genuine smile for him.

He beamed at her, warmth, good humor and relief softening his features. He made her feel safe when moments before she'd been terrified. Jonas looked so handsome in his black coat and dark pants. A glimpse of his royal blue shirt could be seen where the top of his coat was unbuttoned. She had the strongest urge to touch his beard to see if it was as soft as it appeared. Brown interlaced with a couple of barely noticeable strands of gray hair. Alta only noticed them because she had spent time observing Jonas from up close.

"*Danki* for your help," he said, sounding cautious, as if the memory of her fear still bothered him. "I could have shopped alone, but it's much more enjoyable when you're with me."

Alta felt warmed by his admission. "So, you didn't stop by just to ask for my help shopping?" she dared. She saw the smile in his eyes and the softness in his expression which made her wish desperately that she could be permanently in his life.

Jonas chuckled. "*Nay.* I intended to take you for a meal at Fannie's, but since we'd be going that way and I had Fannie's list, I thought it would only make sense to buy what she needs." He turned in his seat to face her. "I hope you are *oll recht* with that."

"I don't know," she began, trying to sound serious while hiding her amusement. "Depends on what's on the menu at Fannie's today." Alta grinned at him, and he laughed loudly.

"I guess we'll find out," he replied, his warm brown eyes dancing in merriment.

As Jonas steered the horse-drawn buggy onto the lot next to Fannie's restaurant, Alta had the sudden fear that the man they'd left behind at Kings General Store might stop for a meal. She had no idea what she'd do if she saw him again. *Please, Lord, keep Abner away from me.* Did Abner Renno live in New Berne? She hadn't seen him for years before today. Was he a member of her sister's church community? If he was, Alta knew it was time to think about going home, because she refused to be intimidated and terrorized by the man again.

Jonas found himself smiling as he drove the distance from Kings General Store toward his daughter's luncheonette. He loved seeing Alta grin and hearing her tease him. She was a beautiful soul, bright and caring, always ready to step in to help. But then she had changed in an instant. What happened outside the store? Alta had been more than a little afraid. Would she tell him why she'd been shaking?

He longed to see the return of her pleasant, unworried self. Until a few moments ago, she'd seemed less tense, lighter. Jonas decided he would ask her directly when he found the right time.

He didn't want to scare her off. Jonas was glad she'd come into his life. With the church elders pressing him to marry, he couldn't help but see Alta in his house, as his wife. He had the feeling she wouldn't welcome the idea. At least, not yet. He needed to spend time with her to convince her to trust him, to make her see that she and he were a good fit.

The street had been plowed, but there was still slushy snow along the shoulder. When a car came from behind, just missing them, the horse bolted and the buggy swerved, threatening to go off the road. Alta cried out, but Jonas managed to get control of the horse and carriage.

Alarmed and worried about Alta, Jonas drove until he reached the parking lot of a small strip shopping center and parked. He turned to the woman beside him. "Are you *oll recht*? You're not hurt?"

"I'm *okey*," she said, but she was trembling. Her green eyes filled with fear. The look on her face was different than what he'd seen outside the general store.

"We're fine," he said as he gently rubbed his hand over her shoulder.

"I…" She burst into tears, and he didn't care if it was proper or not, he pulled her into his arms. Jonas couldn't stand to see her cry and wanted only to comfort her.

She cried for a time, then as if realizing the situation, she gasped and pulled away. Her eyes were red but her cheeks were redder. "I'm sorry."

Jonas studied her with concern. "For what?"

Alta inhaled sharply. "For acting the way I did."

"Alta," he murmured, "you had every right to be afraid. That fool driver nearly hit us, but we're fine, so let's concentrate on that, *ja*?"

He softened his expression as he held her gaze. "Fannie's is up ahead," he said. "Let's head there and have some coffee or tea and a bite to eat."

Jonas fought the urge to touch her cheek. Her skin looked silky and smooth, but she was no teenager. He wondered how old she was and would make it a point to ask her sister when he had the chance. "Alta?"

"Okey," she said, her voice unsteady.

Jonas gave her a nod and a smile. He drove his buggy out of the parking lot and continued down the road. His daughter's restaurant wasn't far. After feeling Alta's tension, he was happy to see her relax as they reached Fannie's and he parked in the back.

When he and Alta entered the luncheonette, there were three tables of customers close to the front window, leaving only one unoccupied there. He caught Alta searching the room, looking nervous, but she soon relaxed and waited with him for his daughter.

"*Dat*! I'll be right with you," Fannie called while she waited on a table.

Nodding, Jonas put the grocery items he'd purchased for her back in the kitchen. When he came out, he saw Fannie talking with Alta, who sat at a table, her coat draped over the back of her chair, in the rear section of the room and away from the window where they'd sat during their last visit. That day something outside had upset Alta and she'd been anxious to leave. Just like at Kings, he realized. Only she'd seemed more terrified when she'd wanted to leave the store.

Jonas approached Alta's table, hung his coat over his chair back and took the seat across from her.

Jonas studied her expressive features, the worry in her big green eyes as she looked about the room. "Do you mind if we just have some coffee and come back later for lunch?" he said gently as he pulled off his hat and set it toward the edge of the table closest to the wall. "I'd like to show you something."

Alta locked gazes with him. *"Okey."*

He ordered two coffees, which Fannie brought quickly. Jonas sipped from his mug then smiled at Alta. "Are you *oll recht* now?" he asked.

She lowered her eyes and stared at her lap. *"Ja,* I'm fine."

"I'll describe the car to the New Berne police department."

Eyes widening, Alta inhaled sharply. "You remember things about the car? It happened so fast—I never gave the vehicle a moment's thought."

"I tend to remember things," Jonas admitted, watching the play of emotion on Alta's face. "Sometimes I don't like that I can, but in times like this, I'm grateful."

"You remember things…" She cradled her coffee mug. "Like what else?"

"After I've read a passage from the Bible once, I can recite it exactly as it's written." Jonas drank from his coffee.

"You have a long memory?" she pushed.

He shrugged. "Some might say so." Jonas frowned. "It's hard when it comes to losing a loved one. I must fight to keep certain things out of my mind."

Alta appeared alarmed. "Certain things?"

"Like the day I lost my…"

"Wife," she finished. "I can still remember the day I lost John. I wasn't with him when the car rear-ended him during a snowstorm."

Fannie came to their table. "A little something to hold you over until you come back." She set down plates with a donut on each one. "I made them myself this morning."

With a nod of thanks, Jonas eyed his daughter with affection. He grinned at Alta. "She makes *wunderbor* donuts. Enjoy one."

Jonas paid the bill when they were finished

with their coffee and snacks. "Are you ready to go?" He stood and picked up his hat from another chair at their table.

Alta inclined her head and followed him quietly through the back entrance. "Where are we going?" she asked once they were outside.

"I need to check on one of my cows. While there, I thought I'd show you my dairy operation if you're interested. It's nothing exciting, mind you, but I hope you'll want to come along." He watched her reaction and was pleased when her lips curved upward.

"My *dat* used to run a dairy farm," Alta told him. "He worked for the owner and oversaw milking and ensuring that the animals had feed during the harsh winter months and were let out into the pasture to graze when the weather cooperated."

After helping her into his vehicle, Jonas got in and drove out of the lot toward home. He was pleased to see the melting snow had disappeared, leaving wet roads and driveways. Alta relaxed beside him, the incident with the passing car put behind her. Within minutes, he had pulled onto his property and parked his buggy close to the barn. Before he got out, he turned to her. "If you'd prefer to stay here, that's *oll recht*," he said, not wanting to push her to go inside.

"I'd like to see it." Alta beamed at him. "I'm sure yours is a vast improvement over my *dat's*."

Within minutes, Jonas had opened the barn door and reached for Alta's hand to lead her inside. He looked down the row of milk cows, pleased with how well his business was doing because of his hard work during his early tough years of being a dairy farmer.

"You have automatic milking machines!" Alta exclaimed.

Jonas led her down the long line of livestock. "*Ja.* Amish dairy farmers have been allowed to use them since 1992. I use a generator to run them. We also use bucket milkers and have refrigerated milk tanks. I imagine that your *vadder* and your family had to do all the milking by hand." He saw her nod and loved how her green eyes brightened as she took in his operations. "I still get up at five to milk and feed them, especially when the weather is poor. Fortunately, it looks like the snow will be gone by the end of the day, then I can release my livestock into my pasture. It's best for our cows, as I'm sure you're aware. The cows get exercise and can graze to their hearts' content."

"*Ja.* Seeing this," Alta said as she continued with him down the line of cows, "brings back a lot of memories."

"I can imagine." He moved to the one animal, who concerned him, which he kept near the far end of the building. "I've been keeping my eye on this one. Her name is Mable. I noticed she had been eating less than usual, and she wouldn't eat this morning."

"Milk fever?" Alta bent to examine Mable more closely.

"I hope not. I make sure she is kept dry. I still clean the stalls by hand, although I hear there is an automatic stall clearing system that some communities use." He grinned at her astonished expression.

"Stall cleaning system?" She gazed up at him, her interest engaged. "I haven't heard of those."

Jonas nodded with a smile. "*Ja*, trenches in the concrete floor built-in along each side of the barn behind the animals to catch the waste. Doesn't sound *gut* to me. I know some dairy farmers use them, but I don't trust that my cows won't step back into the trench and get caught in the steel bars that are part of the system." His good humor left him as concern for Mable took its place. "Do you mind if we stop at Kings again? I need to call the vet."

"Ah, sure." But Alta looked nervous, frightened even.

He checked on a few things and was satisfied with all but Mable. "Are you ready to go?"

"*Ja*. We'll be heading to Kings?"

"We are. Do you need something?" Jonas brought her outside to his buggy.

"I'd like to make a phone call, too." Alta appeared a bit anxious. "I want to ask someone to check on my *haus*, but I could ask to use my niece's phone, but I don't want to take advantage. Esther has a cleaning job this morning."

"We'll use the store phone then," Jonas said after they both had settled on the seat. "I don't want to bother Fannie to use her phone while she is busy at the luncheonette. She takes lunch orders with her cell." He hesitated. "You turned off the water, you say?"

"*Ja.* But what about the *haus* itself? Will it hold up to the cold without the heat of a hot woodstove?"

It didn't take long for him to get to Kings General Store and park his buggy in the back.

"Ready?" he asked as Alta and he walked to the front store entrance.

"I can wait outside for you."

"I'd like you to come in with me. You can make your call first if you want? Jed and Rachel are always happy for any of us to use their phone." He could feel his mouth grinning. "They are Kings, after all, which makes you family to them since Adam is Jed's brother."

"Do they know that I'm Lovina King's sister?" Alta reached up to check her *kapp*.

"*Ja*. Word of mouth." He opened the door and gestured for her to go inside. "You look lovely, Alta," he whispered as he leaned close. "Stop worrying, and all will be *gut*."

Alta stared at him, her cheeks flushed as if she was embarrassed by what he'd said. Finally, she averted her glance. "I'll come inside to wait for you." She looked nervous and frightened, and he recalled the last time they were here.

Jonas called the local vet. Unfortunately, it seemed that the vet he'd always used had retired without finding a replacement. He hung up and wondered what to do.

Alta approached him. "What's wrong?"

"My last vet recently moved away without finding someone to replace him." Jonas felt frustrated. He wanted to protect and take good care of his livestock. Poor Mable had something wrong with her, and he needed to find out what it was and how to treat it.

"I know a veterinarian in Happiness. His name is James Pierce. He's *gut*. He was an *Englisher* raised in an Amish household. He joined the Amish church so he could marry his wife Nell, and he handles large animals like horses and your cow." Alta met his gaze. "You can call and leave a message for him at Whittier's Store there."

"*Danki,* Alta," he said, feeling relieved.

Alta gestured toward the phone. "Call Whittier's Store and don't worry about me. My phone call can wait until I get back to my sister's when Esther is home."

Jonas couldn't keep his eyes from her. "Are you sure?"

"For sure and for certain." Alta grinned. "I'm getting a little hungry. You might like to leave a message on how to reach you on Fannie's cell ."

"Do you know the store's phone number?" he asked.

"I do." She rattled it off to him.

Something softened inside of him toward Alta. He liked her from the start, but now his feelings had grown, and he wanted to share them with her. *But I won't because she isn't ready.* If he was patient and spent as much time as possible with her, she may confide in him. And then he could do his best to make sure she felt cherished and loved before he courted and wed her. The thought of Alta in his life as his wife made him happy. Now he just had to find out what or who had frightened her. And whether or not he could get her to trust him so he could unravel her secrets.

Chapter Twelve

Arriving at Fannie's Luncheonette, Alta became nervous. Not about being with Jonas or seeing Fannie again. Father and daughter had been wonderful to her, and she enjoyed spending time with them. But the other day when Jonas and she had sat at a table near the window, she'd seen her son-in-law, and she feared what Ethan might say or do that would make her look bad to Jonas and the New Berne Amish community who had been kind to her. And then she'd caught a glimpse of a man in the store who looked a lot like a man who once wanted to marry her.

"Is there a lumberyard supply close by?" she asked as Jonas pulled into the back of Fannie's restaurant.

"*Ja,* there is, and it's a huge one called *Smucker's.* The store has everything one could need for building and renovating." Jonas opened the buggy door. He paused before getting out. "Why do you ask?"

"Just curious." She hoped he couldn't see how worried she was about seeing Ethan again. Ethan was in construction, and it wouldn't be out of the ordinary for him to come to a larger building supply store to find something he couldn't get locally in New Holland or Happiness.

Jonas's warm brown eyes seemed to investigate her as if he tried to read her and knew something was wrong. Alta managed to smile at him to avoid him guessing that she was upset or worried. She wasn't ready to see her family. And the last thing she needed was for Jonas to find out what she'd done and how her family felt about her.

They entered the restaurant through the rear entrance, where Jonas took off his woolen hat and tucked it under his arm. Alta looked away for a moment but found her gaze drawn to Jonas time and again. Fannie's place was relatively busy, but Jonas's daughter gave them a table she'd reserved for them. Jonas set his hat down on an extra chair and took off his coat. Alta did the same and hung hers on the back of her seat.

Once Alta sat across from Jonas, she was unable to keep her eyes off him.

"What would you like to have?" Fannie said, her eyes twinkling.

"Are you working here by yourself?" Alta asked after switching her attention to the young woman.

"For now," Fannie replied. "I hope to hire someone to help out soon." She looked at her father. "*Dat*? Do you want the special?"

Jonas smiled. "What is it today?"

"Chicken corn chowder soup with roast beef sandwiches. The meat is fresh. I cooked it earlier." Fannie stood with pad and pencil in hand.

"I'll have that with a half sandwich instead of a whole one and an iced tea," Alta said, and Jonas nodded in agreement.

Fannie left the table for the kitchen. Jonas reclined in his chair, his expression turning thoughtful. "Something is bothering you, Alta. What is it?"

"I'm fine. Why do you ask?" Alta rubbed a hand over her other arm.

Jonas leaned forward, and she was unable to avoid his prying. "You seem worried."

"I fear I've stayed in New Berne too long. I don't want to burden my *schweschter*," she whispered, feeling the pain of losing her family's trust.

"Lovina loves having you," Jonas told her. "She's happy you agreed to stay." He held her gaze, his eyes filled with compassion and understanding.

Fannie brought them iced tea, and Alta took a sip before responding. "She had me convinced at first," Alta said, "but what if she is trying to be nice and didn't mean it?" Lovina *was* happy that she said she'd stay.

"Alta, look at me." Jonas's eyes filled with concern. "She means it," he insisted. "I don't understand. Why don't you see your worth?"

She looked down at the table, while her hands fidgeted in her lap. "I…" She couldn't finish. The bell on the front door jingled. "Are there no tables available?" a male voice said as he moved to the center of the luncheonette. A familiar voice.

"None right now," Fannie said from across the room. "You can return in an hour, or I can make you something to take with you."

Grateful that her back was to the door, she hoped that Ethan would leave and return in an hour when she and Jonas would be gone. Alta felt a painful wrench in her stomach as she waited for her son-in-law's answer. *Please say you'll come back, Ethan. Don't ask for carry-out food.*

Alta tensed up. Jonas had murmured something to her, but she had no idea what he'd said.

"I'll come back. An hour you say?" the man said.

"*Ja.* I can reserve a table for you once one is available," Fannie offered.

"Wunderbor."

"Name?"

"Ethan Bontrager."

"Will you be dining alone today?" Fannie asked.

"Ja. I'm in town on business."

Alta slunk down in her seat, the sound of his voice making her tear up. He was so close and she didn't want him to see her. She had always liked him for her daughter. Ethan and Mary adored each other and had made a good life together. She closed her eyes, but a tear escaped to trail down her cheek. The bells on the door jingled as Ethan left.

The warmth of Jonas's hand over hers drew her attention. "What's happened?"

Trembling, she shook her head. "I'm fine."

His brown eyes narrowed. "You are not fine." He reached out to gently wipe away a tear on her cheek with his finger.

"I am," she insisted but her tears continued to fall, and Jonas wiped every single one that had escaped. "It was only a memory—and not a *gut* one."

"Do you know that man?" he asked.

Alta looked away, unsure how to answer.

It wasn't a memory that made her cry. Something had shaken Alta, and he didn't understand why she couldn't just tell the truth. He'd never seen her this upset. She was trembling. Why? Her strong reaction the moment she'd heard the man's voice as he asked for a table made him believe that she knew him, but she didn't want him to see her. She had sunk low in her seat as if she didn't want to be seen. He wouldn't press her for information. Jonas needed her trust so that she could tell him on her own. He wanted her in his life. If he pushed too hard, he had a feeling she would flee or avoid him. Neither one was welcome at this stage of their budding relationship. Of course, Alta had no idea how deep his regard was for her.

The sight of her tears bothered him. *Why won't she confide in me?*

Fannie brought their soup and sandwiches, and the tense moment passed as if it had never occurred. Alta smiled often as they ate their lunch, and Jonas was relieved—at least, for now. He tried to think of what to do after they left Fannie's and then decided that it was time to take her home. Until he knew what had upset her, he would proceed slowly so she would become more comfortable with him.

"This chicken corn chowder is delicious," she said. "My *dechter* love it, but not my late hu—" Her voice trailed off as she stopped and bit her lip as if she didn't want to discuss her husband.

"John didn't like it?" he asked softly.

Alta shook her head. "*Nay*, I fed him something else whenever I made it for my girls and me."

"I love chicken corn chowder," Jonas said. He waited for a heartbeat to gauge her reaction but there was none. "I enjoy roast beef sandwiches, too."

"Does Fannie make the bread?" She took a quick sip of iced tea.

"She does," Jonas told her as he sat back in his chair. "My *dochter* makes all kinds of bread—Italian, sourdough, rye, white and a multigrain loaf."

Alta smiled. "I was never a *gut* cook. I learned over the years. When I got married, I didn't have any kitchen skills. And my quilting?" She shook her head with a sad look on her face. "My stitches were crooked and uneven. I have a feeling that as soon as I left our hostess took them out and redid them. Eventually, I worked hard and practiced until I improved my stitching. The women in my quilting bee noticed a difference and told me how nice my stitches looked."

Jonas enjoyed hearing her talk—especially about herself. "I'm sure you can do anything you put your mind to. That's an admirable trait."

She sighed. *"Nay."*

He saw her glance at the wall clock and then at the front entrance. "Are you finished?"

"Ja, I should get back to Lovina's."

"Would you like to take home some dessert?" he asked, watching the changes in her expression—embarrassment, sadness, eagerness perhaps to be with her sister's family.

"Ach nay, I've already eaten too much, but I couldn't help myself. Everything tasted so *gut*!"

Jonas tried to pay the bill, but Fannie wouldn't let him. "You'll never make any money if you keep giving me free meals," he said.

Fannie grinned. "You're family, *Dat*. I would have brought it home for you anyway." She turned to the woman by his side. "Alta, it's nice to see you again."

"Same here. *Danki* for a *wunderbor* lunch— and for sharing your room with me the other night." Alta gently placed a hand Fannie's shoulder as she flashed her a warm smile.

"It was my pleasure," Fannie said before she looked at her customers about the room. "Come again to visit us, Alta."

"I will." She watched Fannie, admiring the way she handled them with good humor and pleasantries.

"Shall we go?" Jonas's voice drew her attention.

Alta bobbed her head. "*Ja.*"

He gestured toward the rear exit of the luncheonette and followed behind her as they made their way out. As they left the building, Alta noticed another gray buggy pull into the lot. Fearing who it was, she hurried toward Jonas's vehicle, opened the door and climbed in before Jonas reached it. After he climbed in, Jonas frowned at her.

"Are you in a hurry to get home?" he asked, his expression filled with disappointment.

"I—ah—not really." She glanced over at the other buggy to see Ethan get out of the vehicle and then approach the building.

"I wish you'd confide in me," Jonas said as he drove his buggy out of the parking lot.

"I'm fine." But she didn't know what to say, and she couldn't tell him her secrets.

Alta knew he was upset with her, but maybe it was for the best. She shouldn't allow herself to spend so much time with him even though she'd enjoyed herself.

The ride was silent, and Alta felt close to tears. She didn't want Jonas to see. If he did, he'd be pressing her again to tell him what was bothering her. *That was my son-in-law back there, and he is angry with me.* She hoped this was Ethan's last visit to New Berne for a while or she'd have to leave this town and her sister, just at a time when she was starting to feel loved and strong again. Jonas made her feel like a better person. The last thing she needed was for him to learn the truth and lose his respect.

Alta seemed jumpy and fidgety as he drove her home. She didn't say a word until after he'd steered his horse-drawn buggy onto Adam and Lovina's property and parked.

Turning to him, she smiled. "*Danki* for a nice day, Jonas. It was thoughtful of you to think of me."

Jonas could already feel her withdrawing. He stared at her without smiling or saying a thing. When he saw the pain in her features, he sighed. "Alta, are we not friends?"

"*Ja,* we're friends," she answered. "What made you ask?"

"The polite thank-you for the day we shared." Jonas softened his expression.

"I didn't mean—"

"*Gut,*" he said, interrupting her. "Since we are friends, I'll be by on Thursday, if you're fine with it, to take you out for ice cream." After he saw her nod, he reached to cover her hand with his own. "One of these days, I hope you'll trust me."

Alta looked away. "I know you want to help

me, but you can't. There is something I must deal with."

"And you can't tell me what it is?"

He saw her swallow hard. "If I did, you wouldn't be my friend anymore," she said.

"Alta—"

She opened the door on her side.

"Wait!"

Alta froze in place as she started to step out. *"Ja?"*

"I had a nice time with you, too. And no matter what is wrong, I won't think any less of you."

Tears filled her eyes as she shook her head. "You would," she said. "And I wouldn't blame you for it."

Jonas quickly opened his door and came around to help Alta. "I could never think poorly of you, Alta Hershberger." He reached for her arm and assisted her from the vehicle. "I wish you could see yourself as I do." Escorting her to the porch, Jonas opened the screen door and knocked on the inner metal door. "Have a *gut* night, Alta. I'll see you on Thursday. At one in the afternoon?"

Lovina's daughter Esther opened the door. *"Endie* Alta, didn't *Mam* give you a key?"

"*Nay*, and I wouldn't just walk in anyway."

Esther frowned. "But you're family!" She

suddenly saw Jonas standing behind Alta. "Preacher Jonas."

"Hallo, Esther. *Gut* to see you." Jonas smiled. "Please make her believe she is family, as I think she needs to be reminded how much everyone cares for her." He saw the young woman nod. Alta's face turned red with embarrassment. "I'll see you on Thursday afternoon at one."

Without giving Alta a chance to change her mind, Jonas waved to them both and climbed back into his buggy. On the way home, he wondered at what moment did she start to become upset and afraid. It was in Fannie's Luncheonette. Alta had stiffened upon hearing that man's voice, and Jonas could feel the tension that suddenly radiated off her. What was the name of that man? Bontrager. He remembered that because of their other preacher, David Bontrager. But he couldn't recall the young man's first name. When Fannie got home later, he'd ask her since she took his reservation and would have served him after they left.

What is going on with you, pretty Alta? And he would find out why…and convince her that nothing could change his feelings for her. Because every moment in her company assured him that she needed to be in his life. Permanently. *As his wife.*

Chapter Thirteen

Jonas picked her up as promised to take her for ice cream. Alta had a wonderful time on the excursion. They laughed and enjoyed not only the frozen treat but their day together. She chose chocolate chip mint while he preferred chocolate peanut butter. A couple hours later, she returned home refreshed, optimistic and happy to be here in New Berne.

Over the next two weeks, Jonas visited often, persuading her on several occasions to go for a ride with him for one reason or another. The more time she spent with him, the more she liked him. Unable to avoid him because she couldn't help herself, Alta began to look forward to seeing him. During the days they were apart, she found she missed him more than she ever thought possible. Her feelings for this man were unexpected, especially after living without John for the last eleven years. It was easy to relax with Jonas. Fortunately, she didn't see Ethan again…or Abner. She grinned, feeling happy and optimistic.

This afternoon Alta was upstairs in her bedroom getting ready for Jonas to pick her up for another outing. Looking into a small mirror, Alta checked that her hair was in place and neatly covered by her white organza *kapp*. After a glance down at her purple dress, she decided that she was all set for Jonas's arrival. With a smile already on her lips, she descended the stairs. She heard Jonas's and her sister's voices as she neared the kitchen.

"Have you learned anything?" she heard her sister say.

"*Nay,* she still hasn't confided to me," Jonas responded.

"Well, keep trying. I know something's wrong. I hope you can be the one to help her. It's nice and smart that the two of you are enjoying outings together."

Alta froze as she listened to their conversation. *Jonas is spending time with me because my sister wants him to find out what has been upsetting me.* Tears filled her eyes, and a lump formed in her throat. She felt betrayed by Lovina—and the man she was falling for. Everything inside Alta urged her to escape. Her throat tightened painfully as she continued to eavesdrop. She couldn't hear Jonas's low answer to her sister's comments, but Alta could guess what he'd said. He was spending time with her as a minister so he could help her, not because he genuinely liked her.

Alta decided that she had to confront them but not yet. She would wait to do it when each of them was alone. Moving farther away in the great room, she fought to control her emotions before she pretended that she hadn't overheard their exchange.

He must feel sorry for me. Alta didn't want to be pitied, and she refused to confide in anyone, especially Jonas, who might be quick to condemn her as her own family had back in Happiness.

Retreating toward the stairs, she wiped away her tears, but they kept coming. Her stomach hurt and her heart ached even more for she had sensed a change in herself, as if she was starting to live again. She'd foolishly thought Jonas Miller liked her, that their time together was something he wanted, something special—and not because he needed to pry into her thoughts or her painful past. Alta realized she wasn't ready to see Jonas, to pretend that her heart wasn't destroyed by what she'd heard. It would be too painful to go on this outing with him.

Something he'd planned, he said, as a surprise. And like a fool, she'd been delighted and looking forward to their day, until now, after she'd finally learned the truth.

Physically ill, she decided she should stay home. Feeling sick wasn't a made-up excuse; she wanted only to go back up to her room and remain there. *Maybe by tomorrow I'll have the strength to talk with them.* But not now.

Alta didn't know how long she stood near the steps, her hand on the railing. She started up the stairs. When her sister called her name, she stopped and faced her.

"Oh, there you are," Lovina said. Her sister's smile faded when she met Alta's gaze. "What's wrong?"

"I'm not feeling well, so I think it's best if I go upstairs and lie down. Will you tell Jonas?" Alta held onto her roiling stomach. Everything inside of her hurt.

Lovina's brow furrowed. "*Ja*, go lie down, *schweschter*. I'll let Jonas know."

Jonas was eager to see Alta as he waited for her. Lovina left to get her when Alta didn't immediately appear since she was usually downstairs and ready for him.

A few minutes later, Lovina entered the kitchen with a worried expression. "I'm afraid

Alta isn't feeling well and she's gone upstairs to rest."

Concerned, Jonas frowned. "I'm sorry to hear she's ill. I'll check back later to see how she is."

Lovina nodded. "I imagine she'll be *oll recht* by tomorrow morning. She was looking forward to spending the day with you. She's been happy these last weeks, especially her days with you. If she doesn't feel better soon, I'll take her to the doctor."

"Is there anything I can do?" It bothered him that he felt helpless. Alta meant a lot to him. Enough that he planned to ask if he could court her.

Alta's sister shook her head. "There is nothing to do now but let her rest." Lovina sighed. "I'll check on her later."

"If you need me to drive her to the doctor—"

"That's kind of you, Jonas." Lovina suddenly smiled, and her eyes crinkled with her pleasure. "You like her."

He nodded. "I do." And he wasn't embarrassed to admit it.

"You are *gut* for each other. There is nothing I'd like better than to see Alta and you together living here in New Berne." She studied him as if pleased at what she saw. "Would you like some coffee or something to eat?"

"*Nay,* I should go home to check on Mable."

Lovina arched an eyebrow. "Mable?"

Jonas spun his hat in his hands. "One of my milk cows. I had the vet out to the farm a couple of weeks ago. She seems to be doing better with the medicine Dr. Pierce prescribed for her. I just want to make sure she is *oll recht* since I finished giving her the medication two days ago. Nate Hostetler is interning for me, and he's been keeping a close watch on her. I need to check in with him." Jonas headed toward the back door then glanced back. "I'll see you tomorrow. If you need me for anything before then, have Esther call Fannie."

"Will do, Jonas." Lovina followed him to the door. "I'm so sorry your plans didn't work out today. I imagine both of you were looking forward to your outing."

"There will be other days," Jonas said, hoping it would be true as he stepped outside and put on his hat.

During the ride home, he couldn't stop thinking of Alta, which seemed to be his new state of mind since she came into his life. He prayed she was all right. He had to fight the urge to go upstairs at her sister's and check on her himself, which would have been inappropriate.

Jonas sighed. He'd been looking forward to spending the day with her. His surprise for her was a drive through the country with a stop at a craft fair and a visit to Kitchen Kettle Village. He had envisioned them walking together, talking…and laughing as he playfully teased her about a purchase or her enjoyment of food. Instead, he was on his way home alone to talk with Nate and check on Mable then take care of any chores he'd put off because he'd rather be with Alta. The thought of her sick and hurting bothered him. He couldn't help but remember Lena and how she'd collapsed after feeling poorly before she'd died from a brain aneurysm. The thought of losing another woman he cared for and loved was heart-wrenching.

Wasn't there anything he could do to cheer her up or make her feel better?

It was Friday. He'd see her on Sunday if not before. But he would return to check on her tomorrow, so he thought back over their outings together to remember what had delighted her the most.

Loneliness overwhelmed Jonas when he entered his empty house after talking with Nate about Mable. Fortunately, everything was fine in the barn. Jonas was grateful for the young man who had shown enough interest in the business that Nate was willing to work for Jonas to learn about dairy farming.

Thoughts of Alta remained. He was disappointed that she wasn't with him. Everywhere he went these last weeks he recalled her smiling at him, her joy making him happy and content. If only she'd confide in him. He wouldn't try to force her; he didn't want to take the chance he'd ruin their budding relationship if he was persistent.

Home alone this evening since Fannie was working later than usual, Jonas made supper. He knew how to fend for himself. During the years since his wife died, he'd learned to do laundry and all the other chores that women of the household often did. He didn't mind the work. He would have gladly done it all if he could've had Lena in his life a little longer. But now there was Alta, and he wanted nothing more than to court and then wed her. He'd be happy to work by her side in the house. He wouldn't be marrying her because he needed someone to clean the house and other chores that came with running a dairy farm. No, he wanted her company, to see her smiling face day in and day out for the rest of his life. And he wanted her love until death doth them part.

Alta woke up the next morning after a sleepless night during which she cried and thought about Jonas. Sometime in the early morning, well before daybreak, she realized that while

Lovina might have urged Jonas to find out what was wrong, that couldn't be the only reason he'd spent his time with her. She smiled, and a warmth settled in her chest. Jonas asked her if something was bothering her from time to time, but he'd never pushed her. Instead, he'd enjoyed her company.

Still, what should she do about him? Continue to spend time with him without knowing what would come from it? Alta knew she would have to talk with him and her sister. She had to decide how long she would stay in New Berne. She needed to head over to Kings General Store and make a call to Whittier's Store in Happiness, where she could leave a message for Miriam, John's sister and her sister-in-law. Someone should check on her house to make sure it was all right after the early cold weather and snow they'd had. Fortunately, the weather had changed and become warmer, but that wouldn't be for long since it was November and close to Thanksgiving. Winter would be here before she knew it. Although she agreed to stay, she debated whether she should go home or move on to another village. The thought of going to a place where she didn't know anyone was scary. But was she ready to face her family and those of her community who accused her of wrongdoing that she'd never committed?

But then she thought about all the times she did what they'd accused her of, but it wasn't intentional and it was without malice.

Alta sat up in bed and swung her legs over the side. Inhaling deeply, she struggled to decide how to go about confronting her sister and the man she cared about. Maybe even loved.

Nay! She couldn't be in love. Johnathan had been the love of her life.

A knock on her door drew her attention.

"Alta?" Her sister's muffled voice came past the wood. "It's me, Lovina."

She stood. "Come in!"

Lovina entered, took a good hard look at her and sighed with relief. "You're feeling better."

Alta nodded. "I am. *Danki* for letting me rest yesterday. I'm sorry I didn't come downstairs for supper."

"I admit when you didn't feel well enough to join us, I was scared," her sister said.

She shrugged. "As you can see, I'm fine." Alta took the hanger which held her purple dress from a wall hook.

"Can you eat breakfast?" Lovina followed her with her gaze, and Alta could feel the study and her sister's concern as she pulled out the clothes she planned to wear today.

"*Ja.* How long have you been up?" Alta eyed her sister with worry.

"Not long. Just time enough to put on a pot of coffee and come back to check on you." Lovina picked a comb up from the dresser surface. "Would you like me to do your hair?"

Alta smiled. "*Danki,* but I think I've already taken up enough of your time. I want to help with your morning chores. I can put it to rights later."

Her sister placed the comb back on the dresser. "You don't have to do chores all the time, Alta."

"I like helping you. It makes me feel useful." How long had it been since something she did made her feel good? Her daughters had married and left home years ago. Now Alta lived alone, and although her sister-in-law Miriam visited on occasion, there weren't many other visitors—which should have clued her in that people weren't fond of the woman she'd become after her husband's death.

"Alta, you've done more chores in this house than any of us. It's *okey* to take a break to spend time with Jonas." Lovina sat in a chair in the corner of the room. "He's been worried about you. I thought he was going to run upstairs and check on you, but he isn't one to push or do anything our community would find inappropriate."

Alta frowned as she sat on her bed. "Do you think that me spending time with him is wrong?"

Lovina shook her head. "Not at all." She stood and walked to the door, turning back to say, "Come down when you're dressed. I'll pour you a cup of coffee. There are donuts. Henry went out to get them."

"I'll be there shortly." Smiling, Alta bobbed her head. "And if anyone asks, please tell them I'm fine."

Once her sister left, Alta dressed quickly then washed in the bathroom before she went downstairs. The kitchen seemed full when she entered it. Adam, Lovina and all five children were in different areas of the room. As each took a seat where two large boxes of donuts sold at Kings General Store sat in the center of the table, Alta couldn't help but smile. Then after a short knock, the back door opened and Jonas entered the room. His eyes found her immediately. She saw something that looked like relief settle across his features before he looked away to the other inhabitants of the room.

"*Gut mariga*, everyone," Jonas greeted.

"Morning, Preacher," Lovina's daughter Esther said. "Have a seat. Henry bought us donuts!"

"They sound *wunderbor*."

Breakfast was enjoyable with everyone at the table, especially Jonas. Alta had a hard time keeping her eyes off him and the way he interacted with members of the family. They ate donuts and drank coffee, and Alta thought how right it felt to have Jonas seated at the table, sharing a family meal. When everyone was finished, each person left to go about their day, except for Jonas who stayed to enjoy another cup of coffee. Alta helped Lovina clean up and put things away. She washed dishes while her niece Linda dried. Soon everything was done. Alta looked at her sister and asked what chores needed her to do this morning.

"None," Lovina smiled. "You've done more than enough these past weeks. I think Jonas has plans for you if you're willing."

Alta shot Jonas a look. He watched her intently. *"Ja,"* he said. "I do have plans as long as you feel *oll recht* and want to go."

She looked to her sister who nodded encouragingly before returning her attention to Jonas. *"Okey."*

His face lit up. *"Ja?"*

She nodded. "Just give me a moment and I'll be *recht* with you." Alta ran upstairs to redo her hair and check that her dress wasn't stained or wrinkled. It was fine. Once she placed her head covering over her pinned-up hair, she went downstairs to join Jonas.

Alta grabbed her coat from a wall hook. "Where are we going?"

"I thought we'd take a ride to New Holland to see the sights and then have lunch at a restaurant there that is supposed to be *gut*."

Her stomach tightened at the thought of going to the town where her daughter and son-in-law resided. She wasn't ready to see them again. "Do you mind if we head the other way instead? I think you said something about Kitchen Kettle Village in Intercourse? And I need to buy fabric. There is a shop there that has what I need."

Jonas grinned. "*Ja*, we can go there. Sounds like a fine place to spend our day."

"Can we stop at Kings General Store first?" she asked. "I need to make a phone call." After eavesdropping on Jonas's and Lovina's conversation, she'd forgotten to ask Esther if she could use her cell phone to leave a message at Whittier's Store in Happiness.

"Absolutely." He studied her from head to toe. "You are lovely, Alta Hershberger."

"*Danki*, Preacher Jonas." Reminding herself that he was a minister was to acknowledge that the odds were against her having a future with this man no matter her feelings for him. A church elder and someone with sins like her would never work. Alta decided to enjoy her time with him anyway, even if it was only temporary.

Chapter Fourteen

When she and Jonas climbed into his buggy, Alta began to rethink a visit to Intercourse. The village was too close to her home village of Happiness for her to be comfortable spending the day there.

"Have you ever been to Lititz?" she asked him.

"*Ja,* there is a lot to do there. Why do you ask?"

"I'd rather go to Lititz if you don't mind."

Jonas turned to look at her. "I thought you wanted to go to that fabric shop in Intercourse?"

"Lititz has a *wunderbor* material store as well." She bit her lip, feeling deceitful for not confessing why she feared going to Intercourse.

"We can go there if you'd rather."

Alta nodded and grinned. "And you don't mind?"

"*Nay*, not at all." He drove off Adam's property and onto the road. "But first we'll stop at Kings so you can make your phone call."

"*Danki.*" She couldn't help but enjoy this kind, thoughtful man. If things were different in her life, she'd be happy to spend the rest of it with the man by her side.

The parking lot beside Kings General Store wasn't busy. Jonas pulled into the lot close to the front door. "Do you want me to come inside with you?"

"*Nay,* I won't be but a moment. With the cold weather we had, I just want to make sure someone checks on my *haus*."

"*Gut* idea." Jonas smiled before he started to get out of his vehicle.

"Stay, Jonas," she said, holding up a hand to stop him once he glanced her way. "I can get out on my own, although I appreciate how gallant you've been." She opened her door and stepped down. "I'll be right back. Is there anything you need?"

"*Nay.*" His brown gaze warmed. "I'll wait right here. Hurry back."

"*Okey.*" With a flash of a grin for him, she turned and headed toward the building. Once inside, she asked Jed if she could use his phone. "I'll be happy to pay for the call," she said.

"*Nay*, not necessary." Jed gestured toward the phone. "Help yourself."

"*Danki.*" Alta picked up the receiver, dialed and waited for the call to go through.

"Whittier's Store," a man's familiar voice said. "How can I help you?" The store was a popular place for the Amish residents of Happiness. They offered food items, including drinks and ice cream as well as other things that someone might need for their home.

"*Hallo*, Bob? This is Alta Hershberger. I'd like to leave a message for Miriam Mast. I'll be away for a while. Could you ask Miriam to make sure someone checks on my *haus*? She has a key."

"Will do, Alta," Bob said. "Anything else?"

"*Nay*. Thank you."

"You're welcome," the store owner said. "Enjoy your trip and have a nice day!"

Alta started to leave as an Amish man entered the store. She pulled up short and nearly bumped into him. "Sorry," she mumbled as she looked up. Her heart started to pound hard as she recognized the man.

"Alta Hershberger," Abner Renno spat. "Fancy seeing you in New Berne." He grabbed her arm and squeezed hard.

Her coat sleeve did little to protect her from the man's painful, iron grip. Grimacing, Alta tried to pull away, but he only squeezed harder and grabbed her other hand, crushing her fingers. "Let go of me," she pleaded.

"It's your fault I had to leave my home!" He looked increasingly angry.

"Leave me alone!" she exclaimed more loudly.

"Alta," Jed King asked, coming out from behind the cash register, "is this man bothering you?"

When she opened her mouth, Abner squeezed her arm and fingers harder. Tears filled her eyes as she encountered Jed's concerned gaze.

"Take your hands off her," Jed demanded.

"She owes me," Abner said.

"I don't owe you anything," Alta whispered, wincing as Abner dug his fingernails into her left hand.

"If you don't release her immediately, I'll call the police," Jed threatened.

With a growl, Abner shoved her away with such force that Alta stumbled and fell. Tears spilled from her eyes as she lay, sprawled on the floor. She tried to get up but couldn't. Her injured hip, arm and hand made it impossible for her to stand without help.

"Are you *oll recht*?" Jed asked gently as he carefully assisted her to her feet.

"I'm…fine," she said brokenly, but she could tell that Jed recognized that she wasn't all right.

Jed scowled as he saw the bruises on her hand and the way she cradled her sore arm against her. "You don't look fine. You need to see a doctor. Is Lovina waiting outside for you?"

She shook her head. "Jonas is."

The kind store owner nodded and exited the store. He was back within seconds with a worried-looking Jonas trailing behind him.

"Alta!" Jonas exclaimed with concern. "Jed told me that some man accosted you."

She began to cry in earnest. Seeing Abner Renno brought back the terrible memory of how he'd reacted after she'd refused his hand in marriage.

Jonas tenderly took her hand in his to examine the extent of her injuries. He appeared angry, and she was stunned, as she'd never seen him anything but calm and caring. "Come," he urged, barely above a whisper. "Let's get you home."

Alta tried to walk and winced. "My hip."

Jonas lifted her into his arms and carried her to his buggy. He set her gently onto the front seat and stepped back to study her with worry. "You should see a doctor."

"*Nay*, please just take me back to my sister's." She looked at him with regret. "I'm sorry."

"Why are you sorry, dear one?"

"I've ruined our outing. I've been nothing but trouble to everyone."

"Alta Hershberger, don't be thinking that way. No one thinks you're trouble. In fact..." His voice trailed off as if he was unwilling to finish airing his thoughts. "If I could, I'd do more for you than take you home."

She blinked and met his gaze. He wasn't angry with her. Jonas was upset that someone had dared to hurt her. He skirted the buggy and climbed into the driver's seat. Grabbing the reins, he steered the horse out of the lot and headed toward the road where her sister and brother-in-law lived.

"I'm sorry we had to cut our day short."

"There is no need to apologize." He faced her briefly with a look of concern before he swung his gaze back to the road.

"How do you know him?" he asked. "And why did he do this to you?"

Alta shuddered. "He belonged to my Amish community. After my husband died, he didn't like it when I refused to marry him." She was too shaken to explain further.

"Alta..."

"Can we talk about something else?" she asked, feeling broken inside. Abner had been verbally and physically abusive when she'd rejected his marriage proposal. And today he'd been so angry still that he'd hurt her again.

Jonas became quiet, too quiet, as he had pulled onto her sister's driveway and driven up to the house.

"Let me help you inside," he said huskily.

"Jonas, there is no need to carry me. I think I can walk."

"Wait until I come around to help you down." His brown eyes seemed to plead with her to allow him to do this for her.

Alta nodded. *"Okey."* She waited patiently for him to open the door on her side of the buggy and accepted his extended hand. She debated which hand to give him since she seemed to hurt everywhere.

"Swing your legs around, Alta," Jonas instructed, and she obeyed. He reached in then and caught her by the waist. Setting her down, he waited to ensure that she was steady on her feet. When he seemed satisfied, he let her go.

Alta took one step then winced when she took another. Her hip was aching badly.

"Stubborn woman," Jonas said before he scooped her up and brought her up the stoop near the side door of the house.

To her amazement and thanks, he set her on her feet again before he rapped on the closed door. Lovina answered it within seconds. "Jonas!

Alta! I didn't expect you to come back so soon."
She gazed at Alta and must have seen her reddened eyes. "What happened?"

"May I help her inside?" Jonas asked, his
brown eyes intent on her face.

Her sister nodded. "Alta…"

Jonas lifted her into his strong arms and carried her inside. He set her down and helped her
onto a chair at the kitchen table.

"Jonas…" Lovina asked with concern.

"Your sister went into Kings to make a phone
call," Jonas said, his brow creasing. "On her
way out, she was accosted by someone she once
knew."

Lovina blinked. "Alta?"

Alta bit her lip. She didn't want to go into
what had happened with Abner all those years
ago. He'd not only hurt her physically and emo-
tionally; he'd shattered her self-esteem. Seeing
him again brought back the horror of the days
he'd touched her life. "I can't talk about it."

"May I tell her what happened?" Jonas asked
her, his voice soft and kind.

Her head started to throb, and without thinking until it was too late, Alta brought her hand
to her forehead. She cried out with pain and
heard her sister's startled gasp.

"What happened to your hand?" Lovina eyed
her bruised hand with horror.

"Can you get us some ice?" Jonas inquired calmly. He took hold of Alta's sore hand and then gently rubbed his fingers over its back in a motion meant to soothe.

Lovina nodded then hurried off to make an ice pack for her.

"I know you don't want to tell her," Jonas said. "May I can just tell her that a man didn't take well to the fact that you didn't want to marry him? You don't have to say anything to her or me than you feel comfortable with."

Alta blinked rapidly against tears. "You may. I can't talk about it right now. Seeing him… I'm having trouble dealing with what he did to me today." *And in the past.*

Jonas's smile was warm and tender. "I understand."

"Here you go," Lovina declared as she came out of the back storage room with an ice bag.

He took it from her and set it gently against her sore hand. "What else hurts, Alta?"

"My arm and my hip."

"Let's get your coat off so we can minister to your arm." Jonas helped her remove her coat. When he saw the extent of the bruising on her arm, he muttered beneath his breath.

Alta glanced down at her newly revealed arm and flinched. She'd never forget the iron grip Abner had on it, the fierce squeezing he did to inflict pain. "I'll be *oll recht*," she assured them.

"Your hip," Jonas said. "Lovina, would you please get Alta some ibuprofen? She fell and aggravated her old hip injury."

"She fell?" Lovina asked disbelievingly.

"Schweschter," Alta whispered, "I'm fine. Please don't worry about me."

Her sister stared at her injuries with horror. "How did this happen?"

"She bumped into someone she knew." Jonas's voice was low, husky. "She'd gone into Kings to make a phone call before we went on our outing. As she was leaving, she nearly ran into a man who was entering the store. She recognized him and he her. Apparently, he wasn't happy to see her. According to Jed, he grabbed her arm and then captured her other hand. When he saw what was happening, Jed ordered him to leave her alone. The man shoved her away and left."

Lovina frowned "Who was it, Alta? Someone from Happiness?"

"At one time. He hasn't lived there in years," Alta admitted.

"What's he to you?" Lovina wanted to know.

"He's someone who wanted to marry her," Jonas said. "When she said *nay*, he didn't take it well."

"Alta…" Lovina appeared shocked.

Jonas settled his hand on Alta's shoulder. "Lovina, the encounter was upsetting, and she can't talk about it right now."

Alta gave him a small smile of gratitude.

"I'll get that ibuprofen for you," Lovina said, accepting what Jonas had said.

"Jonas," Alta murmured, *"danki."*

"You have nothing to thank me for, Alta," Jonas said, clearly upset. "I should have come inside with you. If I had, the man wouldn't have dared to hurt you."

Chapter Fifteen

Jonas became more upset on the ride home. He didn't want to leave her, but he knew he had no right to stay. Seeing her hurt had floored him. He wanted only to wrap her up tightly within his arms, which made him realize how deeply he cared for her. He had fallen in love. If he could, he would find the man who had dared to lay a finger on her. What was he doing in New Berne? He didn't know who he was. Jonas had been so busy thinking about the woman he was waiting for, he hadn't taken notice of anyone who'd left the store.

He would never hit a man, that wasn't the Amish way, but he would make sure he was arrested and removed from their community. He pulled onto his property and then checked in with Nate who was overseeing operations for the day. "Everything *oll recht*?" he asked the younger man, who was clearly surprised to see him back so soon.

"Fine. Mable is doing well." Nate seemed to enjoy working on the farm.

"*Wunderbor. Danki.* I'll leave you to it then." Jonas knew that one day Nate would want his own dairy farm, and when he was ready, Jonas, grateful for the help, would gift the young man with his first two cows.

Jonas wondered what he should do about Alta. He wanted to court her. Would she allow it? He would have to wait until the horror of the morning receded in her mind. Then he would take her to Lititz as planned while making sure she had a good time as they enjoyed the day together as friends. He'd spend time with her, woo her, and hopefully get her to trust him so that he could take their relationship to the next level. *And make her mine.*

"Won't you tell me what happened earlier today?" Lovina asked after everyone else in the household had gone to bed.

Alta released a shuddering breath. "I don't know if I can talk about it."

"It may make you feel better," her sister insisted.

Alta briefly closed her eyes as she drew a calming breath before she nodded. "Do you

recall a member of our church community—
Abner Renno?"

Lovina frowned. "Abner Renno? Wasn't he
a few years older than us in school?"

"*Ja*. Not by much. I think he's two years
older than I am."

"Was Abner the one who did hurt you this
morning?" Lovina asked, her eyes widening.

Alta stared into the mug of hot milk that her
sister had made for her. *"Ja."*

Lovina eyed her with horror. "Why?"

Alta took a sip of milk before answering. "If
I tell you, please keep it to yourself. If I want
anyone to know, I'll tell them myself. *Ja?*"

"I understand." Lovina got up and brought a
cookie jar to the table. Lifting the lid, she held
the jar out to Alta. "I think this is going to be
a milk-and-cookie kind of night."

Dipping her hand into the jar for two chocolate chip treats, Alta bit into one and placed
the other cookie on the table. "After John was
killed, the church elders decided that I should
marry again. I wasn't ready, but they said I
needed a husband and a father for Mary and
Sally. The church elders encouraged Abner to
court me. He seemed charming and sweet at
first, but I wasn't interested in marrying again
so soon after John."

"What happened?' her sister encouraged.

"First, I discovered that Abner knew about the cash settlement I'd received from the insurance company of the driver who hit John. Then I noticed the way he eyed my teenage daughters, and I knew having him in our lives would be a huge mistake." She took another bite of her cookie, seeking comfort in the chocolate chunks. "I didn't want to remarry, but I seriously gave it some thought because the bishop requested it. But after seeing what kind of man Abner was, I knew I could never wed him. When he asked for my hand and I said *nay*, he became angry… and violent. He punched me and threw me to the ground while he called me names and tried to break my spirit." Alta took a fortifying drink of her milk. "I was shocked. The look in his eyes terrified me. If Samuel Lapp hadn't stopped by to give me an estimate to fix my front porch when he did, I think Abner would have forced himself on me. I believe he thought that if he did, I would have to marry him."

"Alta…" Lovina breathed out, visibly upset.

"Please, Lovina, promise me you won't tell anyone. I don't want people talking about me. I refuse to be a victim again. He may have had the better of me today, but never again. If I ever come face to face with him, I can't be responsible for what I'll do." She placed her uninjured hand on her sister's arm. Since the hand was attached to her sore arm, she winced but continued to hold onto Lovina. "Promise me, *schweschter*."

"I promise," Lovina whispered with teary eyes. "I had no idea, Alta."

"He implied that I asked for it."

"That's ridiculous!" her sister exclaimed. "You need to tell the police so he doesn't do this to another woman."

Alta thought about it. What if he already had hurt someone else? "I will." She grabbed her cookie and took a bite, but the chocolate chunks were now tasteless. "I'm *oll recht*," she said.

"Maybe not yet, but you will be," Lovina said firmly as she shoved the cookie jar in Alta's direction, and Alta grabbed two more. It was a four-cookie kind of night after the discussion they'd just had.

Alta felt better after two days of rest. Her hand and arm were still bruised, but her hip had settled down quickly, thanks to the ibuprofen that her sister insisted she take. Jonas had come to check on her multiple times during the week. Having missed him, she was glad to see him. Then, to her shock, on Friday morning, two police officers had arrived at the door to ask her about the attack. One told her that Jed King had filed a complaint against Abner, and the officers wanted to hear her story. She'd walked outside with them for privacy and explained who Abner was and what he'd done. She'd also confessed that it wasn't the first time the man had hurt her. The policemen had taken down a description of Abner Renno and assured her they'd do whatever they could to find and arrest him. Hearing their promise made Alta sleep better at night.

Visiting Sunday gave her more time to rest and recover. Alta helped her sister prepare for a small number of visitors. Jonas came with Fannie. Jed and Rachel King with their children were the only other visitors. Lovina refused Alta's assistance with the food, insisting that she relax.

Before he left, Jonas pulled her aside. "Are you feeling well enough for our excursion to Lititz this Tuesday?" he asked.

Alta felt eager to spend time with him. "*Ja,* I'd like that." And she was pleased when Jonas grinned.

Tuesday morning, Jonas arrived early for their outing.

"Sit and have breakfast with us, Jonas," Lovina invited after she'd opened the door and stepped back to allow him in.

"I thought I'd take Alta to breakfast before we head to Lititz."

"I made a breakfast casserole with sausage, ham, eggs, cheese and green peppers," Alta said as she entered the room. "Won't you stay and try my cooking?"

Jonas grinned, clearly eager to eat what she'd made. *"Okey."*

She poured everyone coffee, handing Jonas his first. She took pleasure in watching him enjoy her food. "There are potatoes in here," he commented with a grin.

Alta smiled. *"Ja.* I forgot to mention those."

"I love potatoes," Jonas said.

"Me, too."

Breakfast became a lively affair as Lovina's children finally came to the table and piled their plates high with Alta's casserole.

"Delicious," Jonas proclaimed.

"Tasty," Adam agreed.

"I love your cupcakes better," Isaiah said, "but this is yummy, too."

Soon, everyone finished eating and Alta got up to collect the dirty dishes.

"Go, *schweschter*," Lovina urged. "You cooked. My girls and I will take care of the dishes."

When Linda and Esther nodded vigorously, Alta let herself be convinced to leave for her day with Jonas. Lovina winked at her as Jonas opened the door and allowed Alta to precede him.

It was a beautiful day. The snow was gone, and the sun provided enough warmth to rival the temperatures of early September.

"Are you ready to visit Lititz's main attractions?"

"I am." Alta pulled the edges of her light coat closed as she made herself comfortable for the ride.

Once they entered the city of Lititz, Alta's attention was taken by the downtown businesses.

"There is a pretzel shop we could try," Jonas said. "And a wolf sanctuary if you'd like to see wolves. If this was October, we could have made reservations for the 'chocolate walk.'"

Alta looked at him, intrigued. "What is a chocolate walk?"

"It's a yearly event that takes place before October 12 where twenty-five businesses downtown offer pieces of chocolate to all who enter to shop there. I've never done it," he admitted, "but I'd love to try it one day."

"You've never been?" Alta leaned close to the window to take in all the sights.

"Never. I didn't have someone to take with me before now." The warmth of his brown eyes made her heart beat faster.

She loved spending the day with him. Alta knew she still had to talk with him about what she'd heard during his conversation with

Lovina, but not yet. She was having too good a time with him to ruin the day or the mood. And Jonas had shown her in many ways how much he enjoyed her company. Maybe that was enough.

"What would you like to do?" he asked, his wide smile making her tingly inside.

"You choose," she said. "I'm up for anything."

"Fabric shop first?" he suggested.

She smiled. "*Gut* idea!"

He took her to the fabric shop she'd told him about, and she bought two four-yard pieces of material to make new dresses, one for herself and one for Lovina.

At Alta's urging, Jonas chose what to do for the rest of the day, and Alta loved every moment of their outing including the drive through the countryside and along Lititz streets. They made a stop at the Wolf Sanctuary of Pennsylvania only to learn that to enter one needed an advanced reservation. "I'll have to do that before we come next time," he assured her.

Alta wondered if there would be a next time and the knowledge that there probably wouldn't be dulled her happiness.

"Shall we get sandwiches and then head over to the creamery for ice cream?" Jonas asked, his good humor infectious, making her feel better.

"That sounds *wunderbor*," she said, returning his smile.

The sandwich shop was busy but the food was good, and although Alta wanted to have a talk with Jonas, she decided to wait until later when there weren't so many people around.

"How did you know this place served the best grilled sandwiches?" she asked as she finished the last bite of her half sandwich.

"There are a few of these eateries in Lancaster County."

The next visit was at the creamery where they bought ice cream and decided to relax and eat it in Jonas's buggy. It seemed they were creatures of habit because they each ordered the same flavors as they did the last time they went for ice cream in New Berne.

As they ate in comfortable silence, Alta decided that this would be a good time to be open with Jonas about her concern regarding what she'd overheard between him and Lovina.

"Jonas, there is something I want to speak with you about," she began solemnly as she studied her waffle cone. "I don't want it to spoil our day together, but I need to talk to you."

He paused in the process of eating a spoonful of his chocolate peanut butter to look at her. "What is it?"

"Last week I came downstairs while you and

Lovina were talking. I heard Lovina say that it was a good and smart thing that we were spending time together so that you could find out what's been bothering me."

Jonas appeared stunned. "She did tell me that."

Alta shrugged and broke eye contact with him. "It occurred to me that maybe the only reason that you're spending time with me is to get me to confide in you."

"What?" He didn't look happy. She could see the anger building in his expression.

She sniffed and stared at the window, fighting tears. Maybe she shouldn't have confronted him when they were having such a wonderful time.

"Do you still believe that to be true?" he asked quietly. "After our time together today?"

She shook her head. "I thought about it and decided that you wanted to spend time with me because you enjoy my company as much as I enjoy yours."

"Alta," he said. "Look at me."

She reluctantly met his gaze, stunned by the warmth and tenderness she saw there. "Jonas."

"Alta, I'm spending time with you because I like being with you. I enjoy being wherever you are. Something is bothering you, but I will never push to make you tell me. And if you do confide in me, I wouldn't tell your *schweschter* or anyone else if you don't want me to." He took a sharp breath. "Lovina and I have been worried about you because there are times when you seem so unhappy." His expression filled with concern. "But then I saw what that man did to you and..." He closed his eyes and shuddered. When he opened them, he eyed her with warmth. "I care for you a great deal. It upset me that he hurt you."

Alta loved being the focus of his caring gaze. She knew that he must wonder about Abner Renno, but he hadn't pushed. And she was grateful. She wished that Abner was the only issue she had. Having her own daughters believe the worst in her had her regretting the life she'd led since John had passed. "You shouldn't care for me, Jonas," she said solemnly. "You're too *gut* for me. If you knew the truth, you'd want nothing to do with me."

"I don't believe that," he insisted. "There is nothing you can say that would make me love you any less. You don't have to talk about it yet, that's fine."

Alta gasped. Did he just tell her that he loved her? "I'm not a nice person, Jonas."

"I believe you are." He caressed her cheek with his fingertips but then he withdrew them. "Let's not worry right now about why you think this, *ja*?" When she nodded, he said, "We can save that discussion for another day." He reached for her hand and held it gently. "Let's continue to have fun during our day together. *Okey*?"

"Okey," she whispered.

The tension between them dissolved as if it had never been. Alta had brought her thoughts out in the open and had been honest with Jonas about her concern regarding why he'd been spending time with her. He'd said he liked being with her, and he'd been so sincere that she believed him.

When they were done with their ice cream, Jonas asked her what she wanted to do next.

"Do you mind if we go home?" She was suddenly tired since she hadn't slept for most of the night except for a quick catnap.

Jonas looked at her with concern. "Are you *oll recht*?"

"Ja. I just didn't sleep well last night," she said, blushing, "and it's catching up with me."

"I understand." Jonas picked up their used napkins and empty ice cream cups. He took them outside and threw them in the trash bin. When he returned, he smiled and placed a hand lightly over hers where it lay on the seat next to her. "Let's get you home."

Alta was overcome with fatigue as Jonas

drove her back to her sister's. Her eyes closed of their own volition as she leaned heavily against the door. She must have fallen asleep, for the next thing she knew, Jonas was calling her name as he tried to wake her.

Confused at first when she opened her eyes, she saw Jonas watching her closely. She gasped, her face hot with her embarrassment. "I'm sorry."

Jonas studied her with affection. "What for? I'm glad you feel comfortable enough to fall asleep when you're beside me."

"I—" Her face heated.

"Not to worry, Alta," he murmured with a small smile. "You're home."

Alta blinked and looked out the window to see that he had parked close to her sister's house. "*Danki* for a lovely day, Jonas."

"There is something I want to ask you," he said mysteriously, "but I have a feeling it should wait." Jonas looked torn.

"What is it?" She'd expected another invitation for an outing with him, but she realized that he had something else on his mind.

Jonas bit his lip as if he struggled with what to say.

"Just tell me," she urged.

"I don't know…" He eyed her with fondness. "I was wondering…"

Alta frowned. "Jonas?"

He drew and released a sharp breath. "We've been seeing a lot of each other. I…" He hesitated. "Alta, will you allow me to court you?" His expression was open, vulnerable. "Alta?"

She wanted nothing more than to say yes, but she couldn't do that to Jonas because she cared too much for him. *"Nay,"* she whispered. Then she quickly left the vehicle and ran toward the house, feeling the tension in the air from Jonas's shock. She had probably ruined their friendship. She cared for Jonas. In fact, she loved him, but she knew that once he learned about her past, what she'd done and everything that had happened since her husband's death, it would kill his feelings for her. And that would hurt much worse than anything she'd ever experienced before.

Alta burst into the house to find it empty. Thankful for the small mercy from God, she ran upstairs to her bedroom and closed herself inside. She sat on her bed, hung her head with eyes closed, and cried. Lately, she had forgotten what her late husband John looked like. And she didn't feel as bad as she thought she would. Jonas's image had taken over her thoughts and invaded her memories. Only Jonas. She loved him, but she couldn't tell him. He hadn't believed her when she confessed that she wasn't a good person.

If only she had as much faith in herself as Jonas did.

I've ruined what we had together. Jonas's desire to court her had shaken her to the core because she wanted to be with him so badly. She'd never forget the look on his face when she'd turned him down. *I want to marry him more than anything.*

But it wasn't meant to be—not for her. And she was sure that it wouldn't be long before Jonas found someone else to take her place. Any woman would be fortunate to have Preacher Jonas's attention. Once he did find another woman to court and then marry, she wouldn't be able to stay in New Berne, because seeing him with the woman who was worthy of him would destroy her, and she'd suffered enough after losing first John and now her daughters' love and respect.

Everything inside her urged her to peek out the window to see if Jonas's buggy was still in the yard. She wouldn't give in to false hope. Jonas Miller was a good man who deserved a much better woman than she was or could ever be.

Chapter Sixteen

Jonas sat in his buggy with his head in his hands. He was shocked by how badly the day had ended. If only he had waited to ask to court her, especially when he knew she'd been hurt recently. His hurry to change their relationship into a permanent one had ruined his chances to make her his.

He had complete faith in her, he'd said. That whatever was bothering her wouldn't affect their relationship, that only she mattered to him, but she'd been unable to believe it.

Frozen, he couldn't bring himself to drive away. Alta's reaction to his feelings for her wounded him deeply. *I love her, but she doesn't love me.*

They had gone on so many outings together it seemed as if he'd already been courting her. Jonas had thought she'd agree. Making the bond official wasn't something Alta wanted.

They'd had such a wonderful day together—they'd laughed, shared in the delight of their activities and Jonas had gotten a deeper glimpse into her sweet nature. Why wouldn't she give him a chance? He groaned as he ran a hand raggedly through his hair.

Someone knocked on his window. He looked up and saw Lovina. Jonas opened the window.

"Jonas, what's wrong?" Lovina appeared concerned.

"Everything," he said. "I was foolish enough to ask Alta if I could court her."

"And?"

Jonas shook his head. "She said *nay* then ran into the *haus*."

She looked distraught. "*Ach nay!* This makes no sense. I can tell she cares for you." Lovina rubbed her forehead as if she was suddenly overcome with a headache.

"I don't know what to do, Lovina." He shifted in his seat to fully face her. "I've lost her, and I don't know how to fix this."

"Alta has been through a lot," Lovina said. "She... I can't tell you what she told me. You'll have to ask her."

"Is this about that man in the store who hurt her?"

The woman hesitated a moment before she nodded.

"Her past is causing her to pull away. Alta became afraid when you made known your intentions." Lovina frowned. "Did she say anything else?"

"That she's a bad person who doesn't deserve me," he said, his voice hoarse.

"That's ridiculous! I know my *schweschter*. She *is* a *gut* person with a kind heart." She glanced back toward the barn as if she expected to see someone exiting the building before returning her attention to him. She sighed. "Thanksgiving is this Thursday. If you don't have plans, come for dinner—you and Fannie. Alta will be there, and I'll bet she is already feeling terrible and sad because of what she said to you. I wouldn't be surprised if once she sees you again, she'll want to fix things between you."

"I don't know, Lovina—"

"Please," she implored, her brow furrowing as she became increasingly upset. "I want to see Alta happy, Jonas. You are the only one who can do that for her. There is a twinkle in her eyes that has been missing until you two met."

"Fine, I'll come for Thanksgiving," he said, giving in. Even while it might pain him to be in Alta's company when the woman wanted nothing to do with him.

Lovina's eyes lit up. "*Wunderbor,* Jonas! *Danki*."

Straightening in his seat, Jonas knew he'd get through this. "I want to build a life with her."

Alta's sister smiled. "Ask her about the man who accosted her." Lovina glanced about the yard then stepped closer to his buggy. "I found out something about Ethan Bontrager, the man at Fannie's who upset my sister," she whispered. "Adam has been asking around town about him. A salesperson at *Smucker's Lumber Supply* confirmed that he knew him. Apparently, Ethan Bontrager, a cabinetmaker from New Holland, has an account there."

Jonas furrowed his brow. "Hmmm. Do you know who he is to her?"

"Nay, but apparently he's a young man in his late twenties."

He settled his straw hat on his head. "So, the young man who made Alta nervous is from a place she didn't want to visit." He thanked the Lord that Fannie had remembered the man's name.

"Ja." Lovina's expression brightened. "Her son-in-law? I'll write a letter to her sister-in-law to ask for my nieces' mailing addresses. Maybe you'd like to write to her girls for more information. Something Alta said bothered me." She frowned. "She told me that her girls are too busy to miss her..."

Jonas nodded. *"Danki."* He experienced a

small measure of hope. Maybe once he learned the truth about Alta's fear of commitment, he could convince her that he loved her and wanted a future with her. *Or she'll be furious with us for interfering.* Still, he needed to do something for her, even if it means she would no longer be in his life.

"I'll write today. We should have a reply by the weekend."

"I'm glad you're in my corner, Lovina."

"Always, Jonas, especially when it comes to Alta's happiness."

"I'll see you again soon." Jonas grabbed the leathers. As he turned his vehicle toward the road, he glanced up at the second story of the house before he drove off the property. A curtain moved in an upstairs window. Alta's room? Was she upset to see him and her sister talking? He hoped not. The last thing he wanted to do was create friction between the two sisters.

His spirits lightened a little as he headed home. He and Fannie had been invited to Thanksgiving on Thursday, five days from now. And then he realized that tomorrow was Sunday, the day for services. Jonas knew he'd see Alta. Would she avoid him or be polite and say hello? Would she keep company with women or anyone at a table during the meal after service that didn't include him or members of his family?

* * *

What have I done? Alta stared into space as she sat alone in her bedroom early Thanksgiving morning. She missed Jonas. Five days ago, she'd rejected his request to court her, and it had been four days since she'd last seen him on church day when they'd barely spoken or looked at each other.

Alta dressed and went downstairs to help Lovina prepare their turkey dinner. Her sister hadn't mentioned Jonas's absence. Alta wasn't sure why Lovina's unconcern bothered her. Didn't her sister realize how much Alta cared for Jonas? How much she regretted telling him no before running away?

Linda and Esther had baked pumpkin and apple pies. The family planned to eat Thanksgiving dinner at two in the afternoon. Lovina and she had decided to have corn, sweet and sour green beans, cranberry sauce and stuffing as side dishes. Despite not being hungry these last few days, Alta suddenly found the return of her appetite at the mouthwatering turkey scent.

"Lovina, what else can I do to help?"

"Nothing, Alta. You've done too much already—cleaning the house, doing laundry, making beds." Lovina opened the oven door to check on the turkey. "I can handle the rest."

"I don't mind," Alta needed to be useful, a better edition of her former self.

"Why don't you relax?" her sister suggested. "It's only noon, and we won't be eating until later." She closed the oven door and stood. "You look tired. Why not lie down for a while?"

Taking a nap sounded good. "Promise you'll wake me by one?"

Lovina eyed her with concern. *"Ja,* I promise. You look as if you haven't slept in days."

"I haven't." Alta took off the quilted apron and headed toward the stairs.

"Alta—"

Halting, Alta faced her. *"Ja?"*

"I want you to know I'm thankful you're here with us. It's been a joy to reconnect with you and become as close as we were when we were younger."

"I feel the same, Lovina. I'm glad to have my *schweschter* back." Alta stifled a yawn. Swaying with exhaustion, she smiled at her sister and paused before continuing to her room.

She dragged herself up the steps and to her bedroom where she lay down without undressing. She sent up a silent prayer for forgiveness and thanks. And asked for guidance about what to do about her situation back home in Happiness.

* * *

Jonas headed to the Kings' residence with Fannie. He was worried about the visit and prayed that Alta wouldn't be upset to see him.

"You haven't seen much of Alta lately," Fannie commented as he drove down the road toward Kings General Store.

"*Nay,* not since Friday except for Sunday service, when I didn't get a chance to talk with her." Service had been held at Gabriel Fisher's place. Alta had pitched in to help Lucy when it came time for the midday meal.

"What happened between you two?" his daughter asked.

He didn't want to answer, but she pushed him.

"*Dat?*"

"After a lovely day together on Friday, I made the mistake of asking if I could court her." Since then, he constantly berated himself for taking that important step much too soon.

"*What?*" Fannie's shock drew his gaze to her. "*Dat*, you two have been seeing each other almost every day. I thought you were already courting her."

"I guess she didn't see it that way." Jonas drew in a calming breath. "She must not feel the way I do."

"I find that hard to believe, *Dat*. I've seen the

two of you together. She cares for you as much as you do for her. She'll come around."

Jonas wished he felt as certain as his daughter did. "I pray you're right," he whispered as he pulled onto the King property.

He parked close to the barn and got out. Fannie had made a huge bowl of mashed potatoes and another of sweetened yams. Jonas took one of the bowls, and Fannie grabbed the other before they approached the house. The door opened before they could knock.

"Jonas! Fannie!" Adam greeted. "Come in. Glad you could join us." He looked at the bowls they carried. "What have you brought?" Adam asked.

"Mashed potatoes and brown-sugared yams." Fannie smiled.

Adam grinned. "Sounds *wunderbor*!"

"Are they here?" Lovina asked as Jonas and Fannie entered the house.

"*Ja, frau.*" Adam beamed at his wife as she turned from the stove.

Esther came from another room. "*Hallo*, Preacher, Fannie." She addressed her mother. "Alta will be down in a minute, *Mam*."

Lovina smiled. "*Gut. Danki* for checking on her."

Was she all right? Jonas wondered with concern. Did she know he and Fannie had been invited?

Alta entered the room, pausing briefly with surprise when she saw him and Fannie.

"*Hallo,* Alta," Jonas greeted, pleased to see her. "It's nice to see you again."

"Lovely to see you as well." She quickly turned to her sister. "What can I do to help?"

"Nothing," Lovina said. "You've done enough work for today. Why don't you visit with our guests?"

Did he see Alta's lips tighten briefly before she approached with a smile? Lovina mustn't have warned her that he'd accepted the invitation for the Thanksgiving meal.

Jonas stood. "Alta, would you please come outside with me for a moment?" He smiled. "Just a quick word."

Alta followed him outside. It was a clear November day, warmer than usual or he would have pressed her to wear a coat.

Once they were in the backyard, Jonas faced her. "Alta, I can see my being here is uncomfortable for you. Please know that I'm sorry I upset you. I understand why you said *nay* to me. We haven't known each other long." He studied her, working to keep his sadness hidden. "But can we be friends? I hate the tension between us."

Her expression softened. "*Ja,* we can be friends." She bit her lip. "I didn't mean to hurt you."

"I know." Jonas glanced back at the house. "We should go in before we're subjected to a lot of questions."

Alta's lips twitched with good humor. "You know my sister's family well."

"Indeed." With a small smile, he gestured for her to precede him into the house. The scent of turkey and apple pie hit him as soon as they walked in. Jonas felt ravenous for the first time in a long time—since Alta had turned him down, he'd lost his appetite. He was thankful she was willing to remain friends.

"Dinner is ready!" Lovina called out. She beamed at them and showed everyone their seats.

As Jonas expected, Lovina had placed him next to Alta. Would he ever learn the truth behind her sadness and concerns?

That she had missed him was apparent by the way she quickly smoothed things over.

"Let us give thanks for our blessings," Jonas said, speaking up. "I'll go first. *Danki,* Lord, for allowing me to have this *wunderbor* family as my friends. I am grateful for their friendship and for getting the chance to meet and get to know Lovina's *schweschter* Alta." Alta blushed when he caught her gaze. "I am grateful for my *dochter* Fannie and all of my *kinner* who couldn't be with us today but who have given me great joy."

Lovina smiled and reached over to grasp Alta's hand. "I am thankful to have Alta here with us. I've missed her so much, and I hope that she stays here a long time—and even considers moving here permanently."

Jonas felt Alta's jolt when Lovina suggested her permanent move.

Each person at the table mentioned what they were thankful for, but it was Alta he was eager to hear from.

"I have been blessed to be welcomed in the home of my *schweschter* Lovina and her husband Adam. I am grateful for them and their children—my nieces and nephews. *Danki* for accepting me into your home and making me feel a part of the family." She paused then her eyes settled on him. "And I feel privileged and joyful to have met Jonas and his daughter Fannie." Unable to maintain eye contact, Alta stared at her plate until someone else spoke up about what they were thankful for, then she briefly met his gaze.

"Let's bow our heads and give silent thanks for our food," Adam invited.

Jonas was conscious of Alta's hand in his

as everyone around the table held hands and prayed silently. He offered up a prayer of thanks for the food and hoped that God would offer His help in winning the heart of the woman he loved.

As plates of food made their way around the table, Jonas studied Alta. He still held on to hope that he could win her love. Once he had her daughters' addresses, he would reach out to them, explain who he was and tell them of his interest in her—of her fear of allowing herself to be happy. He was sure now that she felt as much for him as he did for her, but something kept her from giving in to her feelings. It was almost as if she expected to be punished for choices she'd made in the past.

"Eat up, everyone," Lovina urged once everyone had a plate filled with food. "But save room for dessert!"

Jonas wanted to reach over and hold Alta's hand, but that would have to wait. To his surprise, she leaned toward him and whispered, "You're not eating." When he glanced at her, she gave him a genuine smile and he grinned back. Then he picked up his fork and began to sample his food. Each time he met Alta's gaze, she smiled at him…and he prayed that all would work out and he could have a future with the woman he loved.

Chapter Seventeen

"Jonas! I've got them!" Lovina cried excitedly as she met him halfway between Kings General Store and his buggy in the rear parking lot. Her vehicle was beside his. "My nieces' addresses!" She waved a sheet of paper. "Sally Fisher, Alta's youngest, lives in Happiness with her husband Bishop John. Mary lives in New Holland—and guess what? Her husband is Ethan Bontrager, just like I suspected!"

"That's *wunderbor*! Jonas realized that this could be the breakthrough he needed.

"Here." Lovina thrust the paper at him, and he took it happily. "You're going to write to them, *ja*?"

"I am. As soon as I get home." He was suddenly eager to get to it. His future with Alta depended on learning the truth and convincing her that whatever was wrong wouldn't matter or change his feelings for her.

"I thought about writing them myself," Lovina admitted, "but then I realized that it's better if the letter comes from you."

A stiff breeze blew across the parking lot, and Jonas had to hold onto his straw hat. "*Danki,* Lovina. You don't know what this means to me."

"I think I do. You're in love with my *schwe-schter.*" Lovina smiled. "Go! I know you want to write to them."

He nodded. "I'll let you know when I hear back," he assured her.

"And Jonas…you need to ask Alta again about the man who hurt her," Lovina said. "It's important." She managed a smile. "I hope to see you at our *haus* soon."

While Lovina headed into the store, Jonas drove home. When he entered the house, he grabbed a pen and some notepaper, then sat down to write a letter to each of Alta's daughters. He'd start with Sally first. As a bishop's wife, she might be more open to responding.

Dear Sally,
My name is Jonas Miller, and I'm a preacher and a dairy farmer here in the Amish church community of New Berne. If

you're wondering how I received your address, your endie *Lovina found it for me. Your mam has been staying with her schweschter Lovina since she left Happiness. I have come to know your* mudder *over the time she's been here. I find Alta to be a kind, generous and goodhearted woman. We began a friendship from the first day. You need to know that I have strong feelings for Alta, and if I can convince her to give me a chance, I'll marry her.*

Unfortunately, Alta believes she isn't a good person. She told me that if I knew the truth about her, I wouldn't want to spend time with her anymore. I believe otherwise. I don't care what happened in her past or what put the look of sadness in her pretty green eyes. I want to comfort and assure her, but I don't know what's wrong. Something has been upsetting her since she got here. I'll be honest and tell you that we have been on many outings together until recently when I asked her if I could officially court her, and she turned me down. I know that your mudder *cares for me, but for some reason, she is convinced she is unworthy of me. When I asked her why, she refused to tell me and went so far as to avoid me for several days before we saw each other again at Lovina's haus on Thanksgiving.*

Can you tell me why Alta won't allow herself to be happy? I'll be writing your schweschter Mary, too. I got a feeling Alta's sadness has something to do with you girls after we went out to lunch at my dochter Fannie's restaurant. The place was busy, but we came early enough to get a table. Someone entered minutes later when there were no tables available. The man gave his name to Fannie to reserve him a table when one became available. Fannie told him to come back in an hour, and he agreed. From the moment the young man said that his name was Ethan Bontrager, Alta became overly upset and began to tremble. I became concerned when she started to cry but wouldn't tell me why. Alta asked if we could leave, and I agreed. Your mudder pulled away from me that day. We were still friends and taking outings together, but she was unsure and nervous as if something—or someone—had hurt her badly.

Would you please tell me what happened to her? Do you know? I want Alta in my life by my side, and I believe you and Mary are the only ones who can shed light on your mudder's heartbreak.

*I hope to hear from you soon. Thank
you. May the Lord bless you and keep you
and yours safe.
Sincerely,
Jonas Miller.*

Jonas added his address below his signa-
ture and then put Sally's letter into an enve-
lope, which he addressed and sealed. He then
wrote a similar letter to Mary. When he was
finished, he put stamps on both envelopes and
placed them in his mailbox.

With the letters gone, Jonas knew he had to
do something to keep his mind busy. Writing
the girls could prove helpful, but it might also
do more harm than good. Suddenly, he felt nervous. Had he done the right thing? He didn't
ask Alta's girls about the man who'd assaulted
their mother. According to Lovina, he needed
to learn that information from Alta.

Jonas went to his dairy barn to talk with Nate
about a permanent job on his farm and to work
alongside the young man as he milked and took
care of the animals who provided Jonas with
his livelihood.

But no matter how much he kept moving, his
thoughts revolved around Alta and her daughters and the hope that he might one day have
Alta for his bride.

* * *

"Lovina, I need to talk with you." Alta waited in the kitchen as her sister entered the house through the back door. She reached to help Lovina with the bags of groceries.

"Is everything *oll recht*?" her sister asked as she handed over one bag. "You're feeling ill again, are you?"

Alta smiled. "*Nay*, I'm well. But let's get the rest of the groceries before we talk, *ja*?"

Lovina nodded. "I have only two bags left in our buggy."

With a smile for her sister, Alta left to get the last of the groceries. When she returned inside, Lovina was storing items in the refrigerator. Alta set the bags on the table to unpack, putting the groceries she recognized in their usual storage spot, placing the others within Lovina's reach when she had no idea where her sister kept them.

When she was done, Lovina asked, "Tea?"

"*Ja*, that sounds *gut*." Alta felt anxious. Unable to believe that she hadn't outstayed her welcome, she needed to bring up the topic and her willingness to leave. "Shall I get some muffins from the pantry?"

"Please do," Lovina said. When the tea was ready and the muffins were between them, her sister sat and Alta took the seat directly across from her. "So, what do you want to talk about?"

Alta sipped from her tea then placed the cup on the table. "The fact that I've been staying here for so long. I know I've overstayed my welcome. I can pack my things and be out of here by tomorrow first thing."

"Nay!" Lovina appeared upset. "Please don't leave. I like having you. I *love* having you here with us. Why are you in a hurry to go?" She reached for Alta's hand on the table. "Alta, we've been apart for so long. I honestly want you to stay the winter. Unless you wish to see your girls? Are you missing them?"

"It's not that. They are both too busy to spend time with me," Alta said. And they were angry with her.

"You called someone about checking on your *haus*?" Lovina squeezed and then released Alta's hand.

"Ja, I took care of that." Alta swallowed against a painful lump. "Lovina, your wanting me here means the world to me."

"Then you'll stay through the winter?" Lovina cradled her warm teacup in her hands.

Alta nodded. "If you're sure."

"I have never been surer." Lovina beamed at her. She picked up the muffin plate. "Here. Have a muffin in celebration."

Choosing a chocolate chocolate-chip muffin, Alta broke off a bite-sized piece. *"Danki, schweschter*, for your love and opening up your home to me."

"You are more than *willkomm*." Lovina ate from her banana nut muffin. "In the spring, if you want, we can go to your *haus*. Please think about selling it and moving here to New Berne. We have a friend who could find a nice small place for you."

Startled, gaping at Lovina, Alta couldn't believe her ears. "I know you mentioned my moving to New Berne on Thanksgiving, but I hadn't realized you gave the matter a lot of thought!"

"*Ja.* Please just think about it. *Okey*?" Lovina drank from her tea.

"*Oll recht.*" It might be the best permanent solution for her. She dreaded seeing her girls again and feeling their anger about something she hadn't done. That they were ready to believe the worst of her had hurt. Terribly. She hesitated. "How is Jonas?"

"He's fine. Did you know that he permanently hired Nate, the young intern who has been helping him?" Lovina ran water and added dish soap and their dishes to the sink.

Having help on his farm had to be good for Jonas, Alta thought. "*Nay,* I didn't know that."

"Have you ever seen his dairy operation?" Lovina asked.

"*Ja,* he showed it to me one day a while

back," Alta admitted quickly as she started to dry the dishes Lovina washed.

"Is that so?" Lovina grinned at her with amusement. "Jonas recently asked about you."

"He did?" Unwilling to give away her thoughts, Alta kept her attention on the chore at hand.

"*Ja.* Do you miss him?" Lovina finished the dishes and emptied the sink.

"Lovina, I can't…" The subject of Jonas was painful for her. Yes, she missed him, more than she ever thought possible, but she refused to hold on to hope. Nothing had changed in their relationship. Jonas was a good man and a preacher, and she was still a poor excuse of a friend and mother. And he must have realized it, too. He'd asked to remain friends with her, yet she hadn't seen him since Thanksgiving. Alta sighed. "*Ja,* I miss him, but it doesn't matter. There can't be anything between us but friendship."

Chapter Eighteen

Jonas crossed the yard to meet the driver who'd come to bring his milk to a processing plant. "Marshal, it's been a while," he greeted as the driver of the truck climbed down from his cab. "I'm glad to see you. All but one of my tanks are full and I'm still milking half of my stock."

Minutes later, Marshal was pumping milk from Jonas's refrigerated storage tanks into his tanker truck. Jonas asked Nate to oversee the process and to get him if there was a problem, which Jonas didn't anticipate.

He saw the mail truck stop at his mailbox. Would he get a letter from either one of Alta's daughters? It seemed like he'd written them ages ago. Unfortunately, there was only junk mail waiting for him. It was close to noon. Marshal finished filling his truck and gave Nate a receipt. The number of gallons on the paper was correct. As he waved goodbye to Marshall, Jonas thought of lunch and approached Nate.

"Are you hungry?" Jonas asked. "I can make you a sandwich."

"*Nay,* I brought my own, but *danki,*" Nate said. "I'm going to let out the cows to pasture, then I thought I'd head home if that's *oll recht.* I'll come back later this afternoon to do the milking again."

Jonas nodded and smiled. "That's fine. I appreciate your hard work."

After Nate had left, Jonas went inside to eat. When he opened the refrigerator, he saw that Fannie had brought him home a Reuben, one of his favorite sandwiches from the restaurant. After pouring himself an iced tea, he enjoyed his lunch at the kitchen table. He'd thought about eating outside, but it was too chilly.

An hour later, he had cleaned up the kitchen then threw on his coat and left the house. It was a nice day. He walked toward the pasture where three of his horses grazed. He didn't know how long he stood there, gazing at his animals until the sound of an engine and the slam of a car door grabbed his attention. When he turned, he saw two women climbing out of a gray van. He could see others inside the vehicle. As the women approached, he went to meet them.

"*Hallo!* Welcome to Miller's Dairy Farm."

As he neared them, Jonas realized who they were. His heart started to pump hard. Their coloring was different but each woman had Alta's features. Alta's daughters had come to New Berne.

"Jonas Miller?" the dark-haired woman inquired.

He smiled. "*Ja,* that's me."

"I'm Mary Bontrager, and this is my sister Sally Fisher. Our families are in the van."

Jonas glanced briefly toward the van. "Would you all like to come inside? It's a little cold for talking out here."

Mary nodded. Alta's girls returned to the vehicle, and soon everyone was getting out. He saw one man lean over and speak with the driver. Then Alta's family followed Jonas to the house. Jonas held the door open for them to enter. "Have a seat." He gestured toward the table. He watched as they took up all the chairs but one. Sally sat with a little one on her lap. The man who chose the next seat held a small boy on his. The women introduced their husbands and children.

Jonas smiled at the group. "*Danki* for coming. Frankly, I was expecting a letter or two, not a visit," he admitted.

"*Danki* for your letter. We've been frantic with worry. We had no idea where *Mam* had gone." Mary looked uncomfortable. "We had to come. We accused our *mudder* falsely of nattering about something I told her in confidence." Her voice dropped to a whisper. "I had a miscarriage. I said some horrible things after others started to talk to me and Sally about it. I know I reacted harshly—and so did our community." She appeared in pain. "I didn't know how to get in touch with her to apologize and make things right. I love my *mam,* Jonas. It upsets me that I thought only of myself and not her. She raised us on her own and sacrificed a lot to make sure we felt loved and safe—and had everything we needed." She paused and exchanged a glance with her husband Ethan. "Sally and I want to talk with her. Can you arrange a meeting for us?"

Jonas regarded them thoughtfully. "So, Alta believes she is an awful person and a bad *mudder.*"

Sally nodded. "Our *mudder* had a reputation as a natterer. She was never malicious. Mostly, people told her things they wanted to get out to the community." The young woman had tears in her eyes. "Everyone in our community avoided her after they learned about my sister's miscarriage. They felt as if *Mam* had betrayed us."

Mary, too, had tears in her eyes as she explained, "She was shunned for something she didn't do. I...feel terrible about it." She paused. "I never knew *Mam* had a *schweschter.*"

"But then we got your letters. We were so relieved that *Mam* had a place to stay," Sally said.

Nodding, Jonas leaned against the kitchen counter and continued to study them. "I'd like to say a few words about your *mudder.* She is a selfless, giving woman who helped to organize a fundraiser for a family in need. Their child had been hospitalized with appendicitis and had extensive medical bills."

Mary nodded. "I'm not surprised. *Mam* has always put others before herself. I shouldn't have jumped to such a terrible conclusion. Ethan and I wanted a baby so badly, and when I lost it..." She whimpered, and Ethan put his arm around her to comfort her.

"I'm sorry. It hurts to lose someone you love—and I know you loved that tiny life growing inside of you. I lost my wife five years ago, and I thought I'd never find another love. But then I met your *mam.* I love her, but she won't allow herself to be happy. After hearing what you told me, I think she is punishing herself for what she's been all these years—what some would call a 'busybody.'" A smile settled on his lips as he thought about the woman he loved, who deserved a happy life, not condemnation or punishment.

The back door opened and Fannie walked in. *"Ach, hallo!"* she greeted before she looked at her father with arched brows in question.

"Fannie, this is Alta's family… Mary and Sally with their husbands Ethan and John with John and Sally's children."

His daughter smiled. *"Willkomm* to New Berne. Are you here to see Alta?"

"If she'll see us," Mary said.

Jonas studied the young woman and saw regret in her blue gaze. "She'll see you." He addressed his daughter. *"Dochter,* will you call Esther and ask to speak with Lovina. Please let her know that I have Alta's *dechter* here with their families. Tell her we'll head her way if Lovina thinks it's a *gut* time."

Fannie inclined her head. She stepped into another room to make the phone call.

"Is it far?" Mary asked.

"Nay," Jonas assured them.

Jonas watched the young man, who had upset Alta in the restaurant that day, head out to the van. Ethan leaned into the vehicle and had a conversation with the driver. He returned to the house moments later. "He said he'd take us to Alta." He transferred his attention to Alta's daughters.

"Lovina said now is fine," Fannie announced as she reentered the room. "Alta has been helping her with the laundry all day. Lovina asked her to hang clothes."

Jonas grinned. "Alta is always willing to lend a hand," he said, facing her family. "We can head over there now. You can follow me in my buggy."

Within minutes, Jonas drove off his property and turned in the direction of Adam King's farm. As he passed Kings General Store, he alerted the van behind him to make a right turn by using his battery-operated directional signal. It wasn't long before he pulled onto the King property and parked close to Adam and Lovina's house.

The van parked behind him, and Jonas got out to greet Lovina who exited the house. Jonas made introductions, and Lovina looked pleased to meet her nieces, their spouses and Alta's grandchildren.

Mary was the first to catch sight of her mother near the clothesline. She exchanged looks with her sister. "I'd like to talk with her first."

Sally nodded. "I understand."

Jonah watched Mary enter the backyard and approach her mother. Alta seemed unaware of her daughter as she continued to hang clothes. Then he heard Mary call her name and she turned, a look of shock settling on her face.

* * *

"*Mam*?"

Alta turned, saw her daughter and felt the blood drain from her face. "Mary," she whispered. Her first thought was to draw into herself.

"May I talk with you?" her daughter asked softly.

"Mary, I'm so sorry for everything," Alta said, her eyes filling with tears.

"I'm the one who is sorry," Mary said brokenly. "You did nothing wrong."

As Mary drew close, Alta saw her daughter was crying as well. "I didn't mean to hurt you."

Her daughter reached out and hugged her. "It wasn't you. I accused you of something you didn't do. I'm sorry, *Mam*. I've been frantic with worry, wondering where you've been." Alta saw her manage a smile. "You found your *schweschter*."

Alta nodded. "You didn't know I had one, did you?"

Mary shook her head. "*Nay*. How come you didn't tell us?"

"Lovina and I were estranged. We hadn't seen each other in over twenty-five years." Alta closed her eyes briefly. "I...don't think I can explain what happened between Lovina and me, but I know she is glad I came. Every time

I talk about leaving, she convinces me to stay. We were close when we were growing up. Our *eldre* had only the two of us. They died in a car accident when they were on their way to see the doctor for my *dat*."

"I didn't know," Mary said. "I guess as a child I never thought to ask."

Alta could hear the regret in Mary's voice.

"Did you come by yourself?" she asked her daughter.

"*Nay,* we're all here."

"All?" Then she followed Mary's gesture toward the driveway where Mary's husband Ethan along with Sally and her family stood waiting to see her. *"Ach."*

Mary waved her sister forward. Sally hurried across the lawn to join them.

"*Mam,*" she said, her eyes filling with tears. "I'm so sorry. We've been so wrong! We know you. You would never have done such a thing." She shook her head. "I shouldn't have listened to her."

"Her?" Alta asked.

"It was a neighbor of Naomi's—Jessica Graber. She must have overheard Naomi and Ethan's sister Elizabeth talking in their kitchen about how sorry they were that Ethan and I had suffered such a loss. It was a nice day, and Ethan's *mudder* had opened windows."

"I didn't tell anyone about your miscarriage, but I've learned a lesson," Alta admitted to her daughters. "No one would have thought ill of me if I hadn't been one to gossip. I feel terrible whenever I think back to who I was and wonder whom I hurt with my nattering."

"*Nay, Mam.* You never hurt anyone. You've always been thoughtful of others' feelings."

"Don't make excuses for me." Alta turned back to hanging clothes. "I know I've made a lot of mistakes while raising you girls and after each of you married. For that, I'm sorry. Please forgive me."

"There is nothing to forgive," Mary told her. She placed her arms around Alta and hugged her. "I love you, *Mam.* We all do. We've missed you so much."

"I've missed you, too." Alta looked toward her sons-in-law and her two grandchildren. She returned her gaze to Mary. "I know things have been hard on you, losing the baby and all. How are you doing?"

Mary grinned. "I'm pregnant."

Alta gasped. "You are?"

Sally nodded. "She is. It's early stages yet, but she's doing well. The doctor told her that she miscarried because something was wrong with the baby. They are keeping a close watch on her, and so far, all is *gut!*"

"I'm so happy for you." Alta's eyes filled as she smiled at Mary. "All I ever wanted was for you to be happy." She looked at Sally. "Both of you."

"We know," Mary said.

"I'm a changed woman," Alta said softly. "I'll not be interfering like I did when I tried to take credit for your relationship with Ethan and almost ruined everything, nor will I natter another word about anyone." She picked up one of Adam's shirts and pinned it to the line. "How did you find me?" she asked with a glance back at her daughters.

"Jonas," Mary said.

"Jonas Miller, the preacher?" Alta wasn't sure how she felt about this. "How?"

Sally spoke up. "He wrote a letter to each of us, told us where you were and demanded to know who had hurt you and why."

Alta picked up a dress and hung it on the clothesline. "I don't understand why he did that."

Sally snorted. "You honestly don't know?"

Alta shook her head. *"Nay."*

Mary grabbed a pair of pants and handed them to Alta. "You have no idea how he feels about you, do you?"

She opened her mouth and then quickly shut it, as she recalled Jonas asking if he could court her officially. And then he'd slipped and used the word *love*. The man had taken her places, and she had a wonderful time with him. But why would he think it was all right for him to reach out to her daughters? "I guess I have some idea."

"I like him," Sally said. "He seems like a *gut* man."

Alta paused in the act of hanging clothes. "He's an elder in the church."

"*Ja*, so?" Sally said.

"I… I don't deserve him."

"*Mam*," Sally said, "you do—and I believe Jonas thinks so, too!" She sniffled as she wiped away her tears. "Do you forgive us, *Mam*? We're so sorry we hurt you. Every time I think about we said…"

Alta threw the garment she was holding back in the basket and placed her arms around her youngest. "All is in the past, *ja*? Things will be different now."

"Will you come home with us?" Mary asked as Alta pulled her in to hug both daughters.

"*Nay*," Alta said, "Lovina wants me to stay through the winter. We were apart for so many years, these past weeks we've had together—I feel as if we're making up for lost time."

Mary smiled. "I understand, but you will

come eventually, *ja*? Unless that handsome preacher convinces you to stay."

"I don't know what's going to happen with him. I guess only time will tell." She picked up the last garment again and secured it with a clothespin. Alta couldn't decide if she was mad or grateful to him. "Now let's go visit with your husbands and children."

Alta closed her eyes briefly before she followed her daughters. Their visit was an answer to her prayers. She knew she would never again be a busybody, and she would cherish every moment with those she loved. And with those who loved her. *Jonas. Will he still care for me when he discovers the truth about me? And will he understand when I tell him about Abner?*

She could only imagine what he'd think after she told him all her secrets. And she felt sure it wouldn't be good.

It was dark. Jonas had left the Kings' residence hours ago. The days were shorter now, but Jonas didn't care. He sat outside close to the house on an Adirondack chair. Although it was only seven, the stars were out in full force, glorious pinpoints of light in a midnight sky. The sight made him remember how insignificant each person—he—was in the grand scheme of God's plan.

It was nippy so he wore his heavy coat. He'd made himself tea, and he cradled the hot cup between his hands as he enjoyed the silence and the night sights.

Fannie had gone up to her room to read and relax after her busy day. Jonas was alone with no one to keep him company. Without the only person he wanted to spend time with. Alta.

The sound of an engine and the flash of headlights as a vehicle turned onto his property drew his immediate attention. He recognized the gray van Alta's daughters had come in. Were they here to say goodbye? Was Alta with them?

The van pulled close to where he was sitting, and the driver switched the motor to an idle. The vehicle's back door opened, and he saw passengers in the lighted interior until Mary Bontrager got out and shut the door.

"Jonas," she greeted as she approached. "What are you doing outside here in the dark?"

He shrugged. "Enjoying the night," he said. "There are a lot of stars out this evening. Have you noticed?"

Mary looked up and smiled. "There are. I guess sometimes we're too busy to appreciate *Gott's* work." She moved closer and he stood. "We've come to say goodbye. I wanted to thank you for reaching out to us. We're blessed that you took the time to ensure my *mudder* was happy and at peace."

"Is she with you?" he asked, his eyes on the van.

"*Nay,* she's not. She decided to stay to spend more time with Lovina."

"She's upset with me for interfering," Jonas said.

"*Ja,* but she'll feel different eventually." Mary held his gaze. "You're *gut* for her, Preacher. Before I left, Lovina told me about all the outings the two of you took together. And you shared your feelings for her in the letter you sent me."

Jonas's smile was wry. "She doesn't feel the same," he pointed out.

"I think she does. She has a strange reaction whenever someone mentions your name."

"Because she is furious with me." Jonas was afraid it was true. He was glad she was staying, but he doubted that she had changed her mind about a relationship with him.

"Maybe," she agreed. "But give her a little time, and she may reach out to you."

Jonas sighed heavily. "I miss her."

Mary smiled, and there was enough light from the headlights that gave him a good view of her features. "I know that feeling. But I believe that *Gott* has a plan for us all. If *Mam* in your life is part of His plan for you, then you won't have to wait long." She glanced back at the van. "I need to go. My sister would like to get home so she can get her little ones to bed." Alta's daughter touched his arm. "Have faith, Jonas. I do."

And then she and the others left, leaving Jonas alone again in the dark. Jonas's thoughts filled with Alta. He prayed that having her permanently in his life would be part of God's plan.

Jonas sat outside for a while longer before heading inside. He should get some rest; he had a lot to do tomorrow. Nate would be here at the crack of dawn, and Jonas didn't want to sleep in. The farm was his responsibility, and he took it seriously.

The next morning, he woke up after a decent night's sleep. He'd stayed up late and been exhausted enough to put his troubles and fears aside. He did his chores and later went into the house to make lunch. Fannie was at the restaurant, but there was enough chicken pot pie leftover for him to heat up and enjoy. Jonas grabbed an iced tea to drink at the kitchen table. He had finished his meal when he heard buggy wheels on his driveway. He was surprised to see Alta pull her buggy close to the house and park. She got out, saw him step outside and headed in his direction.

"Jonas," she said with a solemn expression.

He nodded. "Alta." She looked beautiful, and he melted at the sight of her.

"I have something to say to you," she snapped.

Jonas's heart thundered in his chest as anxiety took over, preparing him for what she had to say. One look at her let him know that she was mad, as he'd feared. "Do you want to go inside?"

"*Nay,* let's take a walk." She took off without seeing if he followed which, of course, he did.

The day was warm for the end of November. Still, he was glad to see she wore her coat and that he had on his work jacket. She headed to the right and walked along the pasture fence line until she reached the bench he'd built for his wife when she was alive. Alta took a seat and glanced up at him expectantly then waved for him to sit. As he sat down beside her, she slid farther away from him to the opposite end.

Jonas bent his head, wondering what he could say to defend himself because he knew if he had the choice again, he would still write to her daughters. Alta had been hurting, and he couldn't allow it to continue. "What did you want to say?"

She didn't respond immediately. He glanced her way and saw her staring in the distance, at his horses and cows who grazed on the other side of the pasture.

"Alta?"

"You wrote to my *dechter*," she accused.

He nodded.

"You had no right." She watched him as if to gauge his reaction.

"That may be true, but I'd do it again if it meant giving you peace," he admitted.

Alta inhaled sharply. "How did you know?"

"I didn't, at first. But I noticed a couple of things. First, you didn't talk about your family much, and when you did, you got a look on your face that upset me. Then the day we were at Fannie's and that young man came in. He asked to reserve a table and gave his name as Ethan Bontrager. I've never seen you look so pale...so ill."

"My son-in-law." Alta nodded. "I didn't leave Happiness under the best circumstances."

"I know Ethan is your son-in-law," he said, fighting the urge to brush back a stray lock of hair that had escaped beneath her *kapp*. "Tell me about the man who hurt you at Kings." He paused. "It's important to me."

And so, she did. She explained how the church elders urged her to marry him. How she learned the man was only after the cash settlement from her husband's death. And she didn't like the way he'd been eyeing her daughters. So, she'd rejected his proposal, and he'd punched her numerous times and threw her to the ground. Alta confessed that she'd gone to the bishop the next day, and the church elders banished Abner from her community. Alta hadn't seen or interacted with him in eleven years until that day in Kings General Store.

When Alta hugged herself, Jonas reached out and pulled her close. "He won't bother you ever again," he said huskily as he did his best to comfort her. They stayed like that for several silent moments. "I'm not like Abner."

"I know," she whispered against his chest.

"I'm glad." He withdrew and raised her chin with his finger so he could see her lovely face. "Alta, we've spent a lot of time together these last weeks—almost two months. I thought you felt the same way I did until I asked if I could court you, and you turned me down."

"It's not that I didn't enjoy our outings. I honestly felt that I wasn't *gut* enough for you. I'm ashamed of what I was before I met you."

Jonas captured her gaze and held it. "Why? Because you had a reputation as a busybody?"

She gaped at him in shock. "How did you know?"

"Mary told me. You have nothing to feel bad about, Alta."

"I don't know about that. After John's death, I raised the girls on my own. There were times when I was overbearing, like when I tried to match Mary with my good friend Naomi's son. The two had met on their own and formed a connection, a relationship I almost ruined by telling them how glad I was that they finally listened to me and Naomi, Ethan's mother. Fortunately, it all worked out in the end."

"You wanted to see Mary happy," Jonas said with understanding.

"*Ja,* but I nearly destroyed their relationship instead." Alta leaned back and looked up toward the sky. "I'm not a *gut* person."

"I beg to differ. You are a loving mother who only wants the best for her daughters. Mary reacted too quickly. If she thought about it, she would have realized that. I know you think it's because she heard who the real natterer was, but I know she was frantic with worry for you when she didn't know where you'd gone."

Alta had tears in her eyes when she looked at him. "You're a *wunderbor* man, Jonas. Too nice for the likes of me."

"Are you saying you want nothing to do with me?" Jonas dared to ask.

"I'm saying that you should want nothing to do with *me*." A tear hovered on her eyelashes.

Jonas's fear started to slip away as he watched her. "May I have my say, or are you too angry with me to let me speak?"

Alta looked defeated, which worried him. "I'm not angry." She met his gaze. "Go ahead."

"You say you're no *gut* for me," he said. She nodded. "Alta, it seems to me that you're not the same woman you were years ago. And I need to tell you that the woman you were would have still been perfect for me." Jonas touched her cheek. "Do you care for me?" He watched the play of emotion on her face. "Could you come to love me?"

Her mouth seemed to work but it took a few minutes before something to come out. "Jonas, I already care for you. A lot."

"You do?" Jonas's heart filled with hope because he suddenly realized that God's plan might well include having this woman by his side.

She blushed. "Both," she admitted as she averted her gaze.

"Do you think you could be happy here in New Berne? With me?"

"Jonas"—she breathed out as tears filled her eyes—"you don't mean that."

He stood and knelt by her feet. "Oh, I mean it. Did you forget that I asked to court you? My intentions then and now are honorable. I want nothing more than to have you in my life, in my home, as my wife." Jonas stood and pulled her upright. Gazing into her eyes, he drank her in. "I love you, Alta. Please believe that if nothing else."

Jonas saw her swallow hard. "I do. And I love you," she whispered.

He grinned. "So, you'll forgive me for interfering? I wanted you to have peace with your family."

"How did you get their addresses?" she asked, smiling, her green eyes filled with love. For him, he realized.

"Lovina wrote to Miriam. I was thrilled when I finally received them. I wanted to be the one to let them know where you were. And if you're wondering, I told them who I was and my intentions toward you." Jonas pulled her into his arms. "You're not going to insist on a long courtship, are you?"

A small, crooked smile curved her lips as she shook her head. "Seems we already had a courtship."

"So, you'll marry me soon? We don't have to wait long since we've both been married and lost our spouses. I know your girls don't live here, but are you *oll recht* with staying in New Berne with me?"

Alta nodded. "Jonas, I've been a widow for over eleven years. You are the first and only one who has melted my heart. I'd marry you tomorrow if you asked me to."

"I'd love that," Jonas said sincerely, "but I think we should invite our children and our family, *ja?*"

"That can be arranged." She grinned. "But we should wait until spring to wed."

"It's fine by me. I want you by my side as soon as possible." He paused to pull her into his arms. "I love you, Alta Hershberger soon to be Alta Miller."

"I love you, Jonas, more than I could ever have imagined."

Jonas leaned down to kiss her, and he saw their life together as the sun on the horizon, a new beginning, a better life...everything he'd ever wanted.

Epilogue

Spring

The day was lovely with the promise of rebirth. White and pink blossoms covered pear and cherry trees. The rising sun cast a golden glow over the lush, verdant lawn, which sparkled with dew. It had been a long winter. Jonas had waited forever for this day to arrive. Today, he would marry Alta, his beloved. He grinned, his anticipation topped with happiness at finally making her his wife. Dressed in his Sunday best of a white shirt, black vest with matching black trousers, black felt hat and black shoes, he was more than ready for the ceremony. Despite the intermittent snowy weather this past winter, he'd managed to get over to Lovina's to see Alta whenever the roads were clear. With the end of the cold season, he'd been able to visit

Alta more frequently, taking her on outings, bringing her over to the house so he could make any changes she wanted before their wedding.

Fannie was upstairs getting ready for the day. Alta had asked his daughter to stand up for her, and her request only made him love her more. He wasn't a young man but an older version of himself at forty-nine, soon to be fifty. Alta was forty-six, and she looked lovelier than any younger woman could ever be. Since they'd discovered their love for one another, Alta had come into her own. Her green eyes shined with happiness whenever they were together. Her smile was always bright, and her laughter was a constant sound so full of life that he wondered how he could have lived without her if things hadn't gone his way.

Jonas stood at the window of his great room, peering through the clean glass, noticing how beautiful everything looked in his yard, as if nature had decked out the day just for his and Alta's special day. Daffodils and tulips had popped out from the dirt, the bulbs planted by Fannie last fall.

Thinking of Fannie made him wonder if she was ready to go yet. He didn't want to be late and get there after the church congregation. Jonas reached the bottom of the stairs in time to see his daughter descend the steps with a wide smile on her pretty face.

"You look lovely," he told her. She wore a light blue tab dress with a white cape and apron along with her white organza prayer *kapp*.

Fannie smiled. "You look happy and handsome. Alta is a lucky woman, and I think you are perfect for each other."

"Are you upset when you think of your *mudder*?" he asked.

She stepped onto the bottom landing. "*Nay.* She is in a better place with the Lord. I know you loved her. Alta is your future now, and I'm thrilled you found someone to love again. I like her for you. I love her for our family."

Jonas sighed with relief. "*Danki.*" He tugged on the bottom of his vest. "We should go. I hope your *bruders* get here soon." His daughter Sadie and her family had come the day before and were staying with her husband Mark's family in New Holland. His twins Davy and Danny would be standing up with him, which might seem to some church members unusual, but he didn't care. They were good men who had been there for him when he needed them. He hadn't heard a word from his eldest, Joshua, so he didn't expect to see him today. Not hearing from Josh concerned him, and Jonas wondered if something was wrong. He would have to make another attempt to contact him later. Right now, this was a happy time for him and Alta, and he couldn't allow his worries to dampen their day.

He and Fannie went outside. Because he and Alta had been married before, the ceremony would be different from the more traditional one for young people but just as legal and binding. When he'd first approached the church elders about the change in the ceremony, they had given their approval unanimously, as each one was glad that Jonas would be finally marrying again. He and Alta would still pledge their vows before the community and God. The change mostly had to do with the time the wedding service would start. With family coming from out of town, Jonas had suggested they begin the ceremony an hour later. The announcement had been made at the last church service so that everyone knew what time to come.

His twin sons pulled their vehicle into the driveway. Jonas grinned at them and approached. "You made it."

Davy shook his head. "Did you think we wouldn't? It's not every day my *dat* gets married again."

"You're both *oll recht* with it, aren't you?" Jonas asked, wondering why he was worried about this now.

"We think it's great," Danny and Davy said together, as his twins often did. "Now let's get moving so we're not late."

They all climbed into Jonas's larger family buggy with his son Davy driving.

Jonas had mixed feelings as they rode to Deacon Thomas Troyer's house, where the wedding would take place. Would Alta change her mind? He wanted to be her husband more than anything. He sent up a silent prayer that she wanted him as much as he wanted her.

On a traditional wedding day, the morning usually began when the bride and groom with their attendants headed to the wedding venue well before daybreak. Instead, today they were on their way after dawn.

The sun was an orange glow low in the sky as Davy steered the horse onto the deacon's property. Davy parked and they all got out. Chairs had been set up on the lawn, and Jonas gave thanks to the Lord that the weather was perfect and not rainy as it had been two days previously. Jonas couldn't stop grinning after he spied Alta seated in the front row. He hurried to sit beside her, eager and happy to see her.

Jonas took the chair next to his beloved. "*Hallo*, my love," he said.

Alta turned to him with a radiant expression. "*Gut mariga*, future *mon*."

He grinned, pleased to hear her call him husband.

Davy, Danny and Fannie took their proper places in the front row. An hour and a half later, relatives and members of their church community were seated behind them waiting for the ceremony to begin.

Jonas was aware only of Alta during their marriage vows. He gazed into her green eyes and experienced a peace he'd never felt before. So, when the bishop asked if he was confident that this, this sister, was ordained of *Gott* to be his wedded wife, he answered with a resounding "yes" so full of emotion that he saw the amusement on the elders' faces and heard chuckles from the congregation. But that was fine with him. Soon the ceremony was complete, and it was time to celebrate. Lovina was hosting the celebration, and it was time to enjoy themselves.

As he and Alta drove in a buggy together with Davy and Fannie in the front seat, Jonas held his wife's hand and leaned close to whisper in her ear. "I love you, Alta Miller."

Alta gazed into her new husband's warm brown eyes and felt blessed by God that He had given her such a wonderful man to love. She had lived eleven years now as a widow,

alone and lonely, but with no desire to love
and suffer loss again. And then she realized
that as a busybody she didn't deserve a second chance at love. She must have hurt others
with her words, and that made her ashamed of
who she was. Until Jonas made her feel like a
lovely, caring woman with a capacity for love
and the tendency to reach out to help others. It
was Jonas who made her realize that she wasn't
terrible, that her nattering had never been malicious or intentional.

The bridal party reached Lovina's, and Alta
was aware of buggies pulling onto the property
behind theirs. In the back seat, Jonas drew her
close, and she leaned into his strength, loving
him. She must not be a bad person after all
since God had given her everything she could
ever want in this wonderful man.

Davy parked the buggy close to the house
while the guests parked to the left of the barn
in a long row.

"What are you thinking, *frau*?" Jonas asked
her as Davy and Fannie got out of the vehicle.

Alta gazed into his eyes, feeling only love.
"*Gott* has given me you, and I was thinking
that I'd repay Him by never nattering again."

Jonas laughed. "There is nothing wrong with
sharing news, Alta. We all natter on occasion. I
don't think *Gott* wants you to be anything but

yourself." He leaned in to kiss her. When he drew back, he said, "I want you to be yourself. I love you as you are."

She felt the warmth of the sun emanating from her husband. "I love you more than you will ever know," she whispered as she cried happy tears. Alta stared into his eyes, unable to look away or move.

"I think they are waiting for us, my love," he murmured.

Looking through the buggy window, Alta realized that they were the guests of honor, so everyone most certainly was waiting on them.

"Let's go and celebrate then," she said, and he agreed then stepped from the buggy. As he reached in to assist her, she couldn't help but smile, for they had much to be thankful for. She and Jonas had each other for the long, blessed and loving journey together that was life.

* * * * *

Dear Reader,

Welcome to the Amish community of New Berne in Lancaster County, Pennsylvania! You may have visited here once before in two of my earlier books, *Loving Her Amish Neighbor* and *In Love with the Amish Nanny*. This story is of second chances.

If you have read any of my books set in Happiness, Pennsylvania, you may remember the local busybody, Alta Hershberger. The residents in Happiness knew if they wanted something shared within the community, all they had to do was tell Alta. But this time Alta is accused of spreading gossip regarding her daughter when she didn't.

Everyone starts treating her as if she were shunned, although she technically isn't. Feeling like a sinner who is unloved and unwanted by her daughters, Alta leaves Happiness and heads to New Berne where her estranged sister lives. The first person she meets there is Jonas Miller, a preacher. Jonas has been a widower for five years while Alta has been widowed for fifteen. In this story, Jonas and Alta meet and become friends and when Jonas wants more,

Alta pulls back, for she, a sinner, doesn't deserve to be loved by an Amish preacher.

I wish you love, happiness, and good health.

Blessings,
Rebecca Kertz

Get 4 FREE REWARDS!

We'll send you 2 FREE Books plus 2 FREE Mystery Gifts.

FREE
Value Over
$20

Both the **Love Inspired®** and **Love Inspired® Suspense** series feature compelling novels filled with inspirational romance, faith, forgiveness and hope.

Get 4 FREE REWARDS!

We'll send you 2 FREE Books plus 2 FREE Mystery Gifts.

FREE Value Over $20

Both the **Harlequin® Special Edition** and **Harlequin® Heartwarming™** series feature compelling novels filled with stories of love and strength where the bonds of friendship, family and community unite.

YES! Please send me 2 FREE novels from the Harlequin Special Edition or Harlequin Heartwarming series and my 2 FREE gifts (gifts are worth about $10 retail). After receiving them, if I don't wish to receive any more books, I can return the shipping statement marked "cancel." If I don't cancel, I will receive 6 brand-new Harlequin Special Edition books every month and be billed just $5.49 each in the U.S. or $6.24 each in Canada, a savings of at least 12% off the cover price, or 4 brand-new Harlequin Heartwarming Larger-Print books every month and be billed just $6.24 each in the U.S. or $6.74 each in Canada, a savings of at least 19% off the cover price. It's quite a bargain! Shipping and handling is just 50¢ per book in the U.S. and $1.25 per book in Canada.* I understand that accepting the 2 free books and gifts places me under no obligation to buy anything. I can always return a shipment and cancel at any time by calling the number below. The free books and gifts are mine to keep no matter what I decide.

Choose one: ☐ **Harlequin Special Edition**
(235/335 HDN GRJV)
☐ **Harlequin Heartwarming Larger-Print**
(161/361 HDN GRJV)

Name (please print)

Address   Apt. #

City   State/Province   Zip/Postal Code

Email: Please check this box ☐ if you would like to receive newsletters and promotional emails from Harlequin Enterprises ULC and its affiliates. You can unsubscribe anytime.

> **Mail to the Harlequin Reader Service:**
> **IN U.S.A.:** P.O. Box 1341, Buffalo, NY 14240-8531
> **IN CANADA:** P.O. Box 603, Fort Erie, Ontario L2A 5X3

Want to try 2 free books from another series? Call 1-800-873-8635 or visit www.ReaderService.com.

COUNTRY LEGACY COLLECTION

19 FREE BOOKS IN ALL!

Cowboys, adventure and romance await you in this new collection! Enjoy superb reading all year long with books by bestselling authors like Diana Palmer, Sasha Summers and Marie Ferrarella!